SHADOW AND LIGHT

Arizona Raptors, book 3

RJ SCOTT

V.L. LOCEY

Love Lane Books

Copyright

Shadow and Light (Arizona Raptors #3)

Copyright © 2020 RJ Scott, Copyright © 2019 V.L. Locey

Cover design by Meredith Russell, Edited by Sue Laybourn

Published by Love Lane Books Limited

ISBN - 9781785645075

All Rights Reserved

Dedication

To my family who accepts me and all my foibles and quirks. Even the plastic banana in my holster.
VL Locey

Always for my family.
RJ Scott

SHADOW and LIGHT

RJ SCOTT &
V.L. LOCEY

ONE

Apollo

ANOTHER SIGH ESCAPED ME. I POKED AT THE CASSEROLE with a wooden spoon, muttered under my breath, then placed the spoon on the blue-and-white checkered placemat. Dinner was ruined. Again. For the fourth time this week. Kicking my foot against a stool, I sat hunched at the new kitchen island Adler had installed for me two months ago, pushed the dried-up husk of what had been vegetarian lasagna away, and stared down at my phone.

"Why does he disrespect me so?" I asked Madonna as she wheeled around with a puma on the screen—although she sweetly called it a tiger, oh my God wasn't she just the most amazing person to walk the planet?—in a cage in the backseat of a Rolls Royce. Or I thought it was a Rolls. Didn't matter. Nothing seemed to matter lately. A big gray cloud of sad had been my constant companion ever since... well, ever since months now. I sighed yet again and turned up the volume on my comfort flick.

When feeling blue, I watched *Who's That Girl*. I'd always loved the movie but the past six months had raised my views through the roof. "Is it asking too much for the man to get home in time for dinner?" My foot was swinging so hard my slipper flew off, sailing across the kitchen just in time to hit Adler in the face. "Good. Serves you right. Where have you been?"

He blinked, bent to pick up my silver slipper, then gave me that off-kilter smile of his. "Uhm, I was with him." He jerked a thumb at Layton Foxx standing behind him.

Ah. Yes, of course he had been. He was always with Layton. They were in love. I was alone with a crusty lasagna and Madonna, sounding like some sort of queer fishwife bitching at her husband. Ugh, I hated that queer fishwife so much. Why did she keep popping up?

"Apollo, I told him to text you," Layton said, easing into the kitchen, checking my feet in case another slipper went airborne. "He said that you'd know we'd be grabbing dinner after our matinee game."

I folded my arms over my chest. Adler gently handed me my slipper before dancing back out of swatting range. I really wanted to rage at my best friend but seeing him so happy and so deeply in love, I found that I couldn't. I could give him dirty looks though, so I did.

"Apollo, come on, not the Mama looks, please." The big oaf huddled in on himself, hugging his midsection.

"I think I'm missing something here," Layton said, easing around his melodramatic boyfriend to grab a bottle of water from the fridge.

"My mother has a look that can gut a man twice her size. Apparently, I have it as well," I explained as Adler coughed, hacked, and fell to his knees to expire theatrically on the freshly mopped kitchen tiles.

"Ah, okay, yeah, I saw that look when we went to the Lockhart manor in Maine for her birthday." Layton stepped over Adler lying dead on the floor while cracking his water. "She was mad at you two for making pornographic fruit sculptures."

"That was him," I stated, pointing at the dead Railer on the floor with my bare toes. "I told him she would get mad when my family saw a banana dick with two big grapefruit balls on the table among the party foods, but did he listen?"

"No," the corpse said.

"Hush, you're dead," Layton told the dead man on the floor. "Oh yeah, your aunt from Arizona was the only one who thought it was funny."

"*Tia* Sofía is the bomb," the corpse spoke up again, so I kicked my other silver slipper off and it hit him in the belly, bouncing off his expensive suit jacket to lie on his chest. "Oh sorry, yeah, I'm dead. Ignore me."

"We're trying," Layton parried, gave me a wink then padded out of the kitchen. On his way to the bedroom, more than likely. Which, again, was fine. I'd grown very fond of Layton over the time he and Adler had been together. He was a calming influence on the man I called my best friend and the world's largest toddler.

"Get up," I said to Adler. "I'm not so mad anymore. Just kind of mad." My movie was still playing and I hit the rewind a bit to catch what I'd missed. Adler's big hand settled over my phone, taking it from me and holding it over his head. As I said, world's biggest toddler.

"I need you to talk to me."

I reached for the phone, he held it even higher. Given

he was six-foot-seven or ten or something crazy and I was five-foot-eight on tiptoes, I never won this game. I'd quit trying when we were thirteen and Adler had shot up a foot overnight. I was still the skinny, short boy who preferred doting on kittens and baby dolls instead of shooting hockey pucks down the marble hallways of the Lockhart home in Palm Beach where the family wintered.

"You've been super surly of late and watching way too much Madonna."

"Okay, first off there is *no* such thing as too much Madonna." I waved a finger under his nose. "Secondly, how would you know if I'm surly or sad or happy when you're never here anymore?" Adler lowered my phone, his jaw slack, his eyes wide. I bit down on my lower lip. "Sorry, no, forget that. I didn't mean that. I'm just… this needs to be cleaned up."

Eyes averted, I slid from the stool, wiggled my feet into my slippers, and picked up the cold pan of crusty lasagna. Adler slipped between me and the ruined food, blocking me with ease just as he would someone going after a puck. I nibbled on the inside of my cheek, looking left then right, anywhere but up at him.

"Apollo, what's going on with you? I thought you were happy for me and Layton."

Ack, sweet Jesus and Mary. He knew just what to say to make me feel like homogenized shit. I drew in a deep breath, tipped my head back a bit, and gazed at the redhead who was my brother in every aspect other than sharing the same blood. A brother from another mother. And father.

"I am happy for you. *I am!*" I insisted when his eyebrows knitted. "I am really happy for you, honestly. It's

not you, it's me. I'm not happy with *me* anymore." I
thumped my chest. "I'm just…" I searched for the right
word to fit my mood. "Stagnant. Lonely. Unneeded.
Unwanted."

"Whoa, just whoa. You are most certainly needed and
wanted, please don't *ever* think you're not. Who else
would put up with my stupid shit on a daily basis?"

"Layton," I whispered as Griffin Dunne and Madonna
exchanged witty banter.

His wide shoulders sunk a bit before he handed me my
phone. I glanced down at my cell to pause the movie.

"I'm sorry you're lonely, Apollo. We can come over
here more. I know we spend a lot of time at Layton's but
he's kind of more comfortable there, but I can insist
that we—"

"No, no, no." I slid around him, grabbing the pan of
congealed noodles, cheese, and sauce and carrying it to the
sink. "Do not make him do anything. He's sensitive. If he's
happier at his place, go to his place. This is all on me." I
grabbed a knife from the sink and started chipping at the
crusty mess.

"Maybe you should try dating more." I threw him
another Mama look that made the big man draw back a
step. "It's been a year since… he who must not be named.
Maybe I can set you up with one of the guys on the team."

"There *are* no gay or bi men on the Railers that aren't
spoken for, Adler. And I don't want to have you set me
up. I'm a fucking fabulous Latino queer man and I'm
quite capable of finding my own dates, thank you very
much. Stupid fucking cheese!" I stabbed violently at the
mess in the pan. "And do *not* bring up Jean-Claude

again, even in passing and with a fake name! That cheating, pig-faced jackass! I will *never* cheer for that stupid team ever again! Sweet-talking French goalies are heartbreakers!"

"Sorry, okay, I just don't know what to do for you. Can you stop assaulting that poor food?"

I paused, breathless, and stared down at the carnage. "Oh man, my lasagna." I dropped the butter knife and the pan into the sink. Then I covered my face with a sauce-speckled hand. "I'm just not happy anymore, Adler."

One large hand settled on my shoulder, then another on the other shoulder. I shook my head but he spun me around with ease, the big pushy asshole.

"What *will* make you happy?"

"I don't know. I want someone to want me, to need me, to love me."

"*I* love you," he said, pulling me in for a big, brotherly hug that felt so good I started crying like that soap opera star Mama adored. That woman could weep at the drop of a hat. Seemed I could too, but my tears were brought on by food murder.

"I know, and I love you too, but that's brotherly love. I want…" I mumbled into his silk shirt then paused. What did I want? "I want someone of my own, Adler. Someone who'll look at me as you look at Layton. I want something strong, real, happy. I want to feel happy again. I want to be needed."

"*I* need you."

"Not like you did before." I wrapped my arms around him and held him. "You found your future; I think maybe it's time I found mine."

He pulled back to gaze at me. His eyes were dewy. God damn me for making everything so fucking dramatic.

"Can it be here in Harrisburg? I'm not sure I can function if you're not here at my side. We've been together since we were kids. I remember toddling around the Maine mansion with you, running outside with Nanny trying to keep up, making mud pies then serving them to my parents when they dropped in. Oh! And that time we snuck out when we were ten to go see that horror movie. We slept together for four months afterwards. Stupid fucking shaky-headed demon women still freak me out."

I smiled, a reedy smile yes, but it was a smile. "I remember all of that, and I treasure each of those memories. Well, not the shaky-head demon woman, I still can't do those, but everything else. I'm just lost, I guess. I've built my life around you and now you don't need me." I gasped. "I sound like Mama!"

Adler chuckled, pulled me tight to his chest, and then pecked my hair affectionately. "You really do, but I get it. We'll work on making you happy again. I can't have my little brother unhappy. Would you like a new car?"

"Stop," I said on a weak laugh, my nose pressed into his shoulder.

"A boat? Boats make people happy. You can float a boat."

"Stop."

"Oh! How about the entire Madonna musical collection? Oh wait, you already own that."

"*Stop.* What I want can't be bought." I squeezed his middle then broke free, wiping at my face as I stepped back. "I'm not sure what it is I *do* want, but it's deeper than presents and expensive gifts. I want…" I threw up my hands in exasperation.

Adler gave me a sad smile. "We'll figure out what it is you want and when we do I'll move heaven and earth to give it to you. *Mi hermano*."

My brother. I choked up again then waved him out of my kitchen so I could clean up the mess I'd made out of myself and supper. The pan would need soaking but it'd survive, just a bit more scarred than it had been before. There was some sort of life metaphor or something in that last thought.

"Be the pan, Apollo," I whispered to the empty room. Great, now I was patterning my life after bakeware. I really did need to figure out who I was and where the hell I was going. I'd not be able to focus well on an empty stomach or without the queen of pop, though. I'd think better after more Madonna and some chocolate-marshmallow ice cream. Obvs.

THE NEXT MORNING WAS A BLEAK ONE IN HARRISBURG. The March sky had been dark gray when I woke up, threatening winter fury. As the three of us were eating breakfast, the fury arrived in the form of freezing rain that crippled the city in an hour. Schools were cancelled, office and government workers given the day off, and the Railers morning skate had been scrapped. The game tonight—one of a back-to-back—was still on as far as we knew. It was an in-state game with Philadelphia, so maybe with the bad weather Trent's Lola would stay home. We all loved the figure skater's grandmother but she was brutal at times. Talk about a rabid fan.

Layton and Adler lounged around in bed after breakfast. I cleaned up, ran the vacuum, and then sat at the desk by the window and stared out at the icy landscape of Harrisburg, my light therapy box on and shining on my face. For several years the box had worked pretty well, keeping me off meds for the seasonal funk I'd always fallen into. This year though…

Rain hit the windows and froze. My mind wandered aimlessly. Winter weather sucked, it truly did. It was depressing the shit out of me. I snuggled into my thick sweater, wishing I were somewhere warm and sunny. Tucking my legs up under me, I sat there until someone lobbed a stuffed lobster at me. It missed, hit the icy window, and fell to the desk where it tipped over a cup filled with pens.

I didn't even have to look to know who was responsible.

"Sorry, that was supposed to hit you in the head then I was going to yell something incredibly funny like, 'Is that a lobster on your head or are you just happy to see me?' but I missed and the whole joke is shot in the ass. So, hey, what are you doing?" Adler bounded over to the desk and gathered up his stuffed lobster, which he held to his bare chest. At least he had pulled on lounge pants. Sometimes he didn't.

"Watching the world freeze."

"Man, your SAD is really bad this year." He took the back of the chair in his hands then rolled me from the window to the living room where he parked me then sat on the sofa. His ginger hair was knotted from sleep or sex, probably both given that I'd not seen Layton since we'd had breakfast. Adler had more than likely loved his man back to sleep. I so wasn't envious of the two of them. Okay, yes, I was, and I hated that I was. "So, I was checking in on how Henry is doing."

"How is he?"

"Doing okay. The leg is slow and his vision is still not where it should be, but they're all hopeful. Anyway, I'm letting him stay at my new property in Tucson. He's being released tomorrow and he's on his own. He'll be looking for someone to move in and take care of him. Clean, cook, drive him to his rehab and doctor's appointments."

"So they're looking for someone to provide home care. I'm not a nurse." I wasn't sure what I was. Adler Lockhart's… what exactly? Personal assistant? Yes, that had always fit when people asked what I did. Add baby-sitter, errand boy, keeper of important facts, chief cook and bottlewasher, and shoulder to cry on and this was a fair idea of my job/life. It revolved around Adler and always had. I loved him but was that good? I didn't have a clue about anything aside from having chilly feet. My toes were icy cold as they peeked out from under my funky, retro bell-bottom jeans. I needed to find my slippers.

"No, he has a nurse coming in twice a week. He needs someone to live there with him on a temporary basis. A companion. I told his brother Dan that I'd ask you."

My gaze flew from my cold tan toes—I needed a pedicure badly as my bright pink polish was chipped to shit—to Adler. He was the picture of earnest affection. Layton liked to say he reminded him of an Irish Setter—all red and pretty and exuberant and overeager to please. That comparison fit perfectly.

"Me? But I have a job as your handler."

He snorted in amusement but the humor quickly faded. "Yeah, a job that you're not happy with anymore." He looked down at the stuffed lobster, a memento he'd brought home from a cruise he and Layton had taken last summer. The summer I'd been seeing that rat bastard Jean-Claude. I spit on his memory in my mind. "You don't have to even think about it if you don't want to. I'd be super happy if you stayed here but you're just so damn sad, and I feel like shit for ignoring you to be with Layton."

"*Adler…*"

"I just thought that maybe this might be a solution. Get away from the cold weather which I know you hate, visit your Aunt Sofía, hang out with Henry, who's a nice guy who also had a disastrous relationship with a real dick-bag shithead. Work on your tan, cook food for someone who will be there to eat it, maybe make some new friends and go out, fall in love. I want you to be happy even if it kills me to see you leave."

I gave my head a shake. No. This wasn't what I wanted. "I don't want to leave you here alone."

"But that's just it, I won't *be* alone. I have Layton." He reached out to place his hand on my exposed toes. "Your toes are like ice. Dude, find your slippers then have a think, okay? It's not for ever, just until Henry is back to his normal life. Maybe three months or so? I'm sure I can manage on my own for three months." My right eyebrow climbed up my brow. "I totally can be a grown-up if I have to be."

"Do you want me to go?"

His warm hand on my cold toes felt so good. He squeezed my smallest toe playfully then gave it a tug. "No, Apollo, I don't want you to go. I want you to be here to take care of all the shitty things about life that I like to ignore. But that's not fair to you when you're obviously unhappy with your life now."

"You've been talking to Layton about this, haven't you?" I adored Adler but his upbringing made him a little blind to those around him at times. Being so rich and so spoiled, he tended to only see the brightest star in the sky, which was him. Adler was the sun and we were just little piddle planets caught in his gravitational pull.

"No, actually, I haven't. Well, not about the thing with Henry. That was all me. He just suggested I try to look past my wants and needs to focus on yours, for a change." He gave me that Adler Lockhart look. The one that said he knew he could be self-centered at times but he didn't mean to be, which he didn't. Adler would buy anyone anything they asked for. Sometimes, though, what a person needed couldn't be purchased. "It was just a thought. Why don't you think about it. I'm going back to bed. You can keep Rocky."

He stood then handed me the plush red lobster. "Rocky for the B-52's song?"

His goofy smile lit up his face. "You know me too well."

Off he went to his lover. Using one foot, I rolled back to the desk, over a few pens that needed to be picked up, Rocky tucked under my arm, and resumed my moment of reflection. The rain was mixed with snow now. The charcoal sky was throwing everything it had at Harrisburg. The March storm was a sound kick in the balls for those of us who lived for summer. Spring had been so close, just a few weeks away, hiding in April.

It's warm in Arizona, Apollo, and sunny. There's someone who needs you out there too. Someone who's been broken by love just like you. Someone who's struggling to find himself just like you.

The soft sound of male laughter floated over me. Maybe it *was* time to seek out the sun. God knows living in the shadows wasn't for me and my brilliantly queer Latino light.

TWO

Henry

———

"IT'S A COMPROMISE, BUT THE LOWER CASH AMOUNT
would solve a lot of your current issues, Henry." Oscar
Bledford, lawyer extraordinaire, was all kinds of earnest,
leaning forward in his chair and visibly buzzing with
excitement. I didn't really like him much, but then it
seemed I was right not to like him, let alone trust him.
Next to him was the stony-faced Keith Jazz from AZK
Insurance who, let's face it, was far from jazzed that his
company had to pay out one-point-seven million on my
claim.

I didn't even know I'd been insured, but then, I didn't
know a lot about anything; that much had become evident
over the last few months. This particular policy was one
my mom had taken out for me, and one of the only things
she'd kept up religiously. Unfortunately, it was the lone
bright spot on the horizon, because Mom and my wannabe
step-dad, Ed, had taken everything else from me in deals
and investments and spending on things they couldn't
afford. They'd burned through the money she'd inherited

from Dad, and then moved onto my trust fund and then my income, just as fast.

"Career-ending?" I blinked at the man who never gave me anything but bad news, and wondered if he had any idea what he was talking about. "You genuinely think that my career is only worth that much?"

He nodded so fast I thought he'd give himself a concussion. "It would clear most of your debts, get you to a point where you can find something else, start again." He looked so damned triumphant and all I wanted to do was slam his face into a wall. Of course, I wasn't capable of standing upright without tripping over my own feet, and I'd probably forget why I was pushing him into a wall by the time I got there, but the anger worked to focus my thoughts. Starting over? As what? I didn't have a degree as some of the other guys on the team. I'd played hockey since before I could recall, and it was my life. I'd been drafted, I'd had a place on several AHL teams, then I'd been traded to the Raptors feeder team, the Sierra Vista Skylarks, and yeah, I get the Raptors were the dregs of the NHL, but fuck, they *were* an actual NHL team, and they'd wanted me.

Hardworking, desperate to please, easygoing Henry. I was fast; faster even than Ryker off the corner, and that was saying something given how much of a wonder boy he'd become with his adulation and his goals and his pretty face.

Fuck.

I curled my hands into fists on my lap, and dug my nails in, the prick of pain anchoring me to the scene in the room. I was good, and if I got back on the ice I could earn way more than this money they were throwing at me now. Was the payment just proof that I was finished, because of a fucked-up leg and an eye that wouldn't work? I was still on the Raptors team, just on long-term injured reserve. No one had said anything about me being thrown off.

I wished I had someone there with me, to hold my hand, metaphorically at least. This time last year my agent would have been by my side. Lewis McCourt had nurtured me through juniors as a friend and then pushed me to be the best all through my time in the AHL and right up into the Raptors. But he wasn't going to be there, was he, another satellite in the orbit of Ed and my mom with their stealing and lying.

I wish I could recall exactly why he'd left, only knowing that Mom had told me, she and her current boyfriend Ed, that I deserved better, and I'd believed her. She was my mom, why wouldn't I believe her? Now my agent was gone, my new agent didn't really know me, and Rob had taken over so much, telling me I didn't have to worry and that he and my mom had things fixed. But look at me now. I'd lost everything, and in addition to the loss, it seemed I had a line of people wanting to sue me.

"You should take the insurance payout offer, Henry," Oscar encouraged. "Take the weight off your shoulders, focus on healing, maybe get a job and work off the rest on a payment schedule? You wouldn't have to leave hockey. You could take an admin role, or charity management or something." He waved his hand to embellish the *something* part of that, and looked so happy with his suggestions.

My head might have been muddled, but I wasn't

stupid. If I took this offer, he'd want it all, and I doubted many of my creditors would be paid off. I closed my eyes momentarily, just so I didn't have to see the faces opposite me across this wide desk, telling me what to do for the best. They saw the end of my life as a hockey player, and to both of them this money was a career-ending settlement. The insurance company had already negotiated down from the full six million, stating a hundred terms that I had somehow unknowingly violated.

You did get in the car. You knew Aarni was on the edge. You brought this on yourself. It's mostly your fault.

I'd heard it all before, in whispered conversations between care professionals, my mom in her last vitriolic attack on me, and right here in this room where the company who'd insured me had decided I wasn't worth more.

"Losing a career as a hockey player is worth more than what you're offering."

Keith opened his mouth to bluster on behalf of AZK, but Oscar was the first to talk.

"You were with a team." He peered at his phone as if he needed to remind himself of how much I'd fucked up. "The Raptors are an unsustainable franchise by all accounts, and I have a suggestion from certain teammates here that you were close to being sent down to the minors."

Who said that? Aarni? Ryker? Alex? Coach? I don't recall anyone saying I was being sent down? I don't remember Coach Carmichael telling me I wasn't pulling my weight. I wish he was here. Maybe I'm wrong. Maybe I don't remember this right.

I pressed fingers to my temples, and stumbled to stand. "I need a few minutes," I blurted and headed out of the room, knocked into a small table as I went, struggled to focus on finding the door handle. Finally, mercifully, I was out in the hallway, and then I didn't know what else to do. Should I get out of here or go back and talk some more? I wasn't a quitter, I should go back, so I headed for the bathrooms to give myself breathing time, then locked myself in a cubicle. I sat on the closed toilet, head bowed, my left hand shaking so much I had to hold it still, and my leg throbbing from thigh to knee. I felt dizzy, uncoordinated, and I had a big decisions to make.

Mom and Ed had taken everything. It had started small, transfers between my accounts, robbing from one to pay the other, nothing I would ever notice because, *fuck*, this was my mom, and Ed seemed like a good guy who made her smile, and I was playing the game I loved. In fact, everything was a garden of freaking roses. She took care of me, he watched over my finances, and as long as my account had enough to pay rent and bills I never cared.

I should have showed more interest. I should never have blindly trusted her or Ed. Or thought for one minute that mom had my back.

When they took others' money in my name, I was told it was endorsements, that I should sign, and I never checked. Grief tightened in my chest with the complete stupidity I'd shown, and I closed my eyes as it overpowered me and left me shaking again. With my eyes shut I couldn't see the dark floaters in my left eye, or imagine the awful damage to my retina that no one could see from the outside. Too many specialists had looked at me, all covered by the team, and not one of them had told me anything I wanted to hear.

I'd climbed into a car with a man whose temper was high, a man who'd used me, hurt me, and nearly killed me. He'd walked away from the accident. Experts had said he'd turned the wheel so the brunt of the hit was on my side. I don't recall any of that, and that was the sole blessing with my fucked-up brain. My leg would heal, the titanium rod was the least of my worries, and one day with the PT I was having, I could be back on the ice and able to skate. But to play again? That wasn't so definite because it was my vision that was messed up. The accident had been so bad that I had to be cut from the car, my leg pinned, my face embedded in the window. As I recalled what I could, I traced the scar I would forever carry under the hair that had only just begun to grow back properly. Concussion, and being in a coma for a while had been the start of things. Waking up was the start of my living nightmare. My right eye had been severely slashed on the sclera, which had resulted in a torn and detached retina. I was mostly blind in one eye and everything for which I'd worked my entire life was gone.

Four experts had assessed my injuries. Three told me I was done. Only one had offered any hope, but added that the odds were low.

All I recalled was telling Ryker and Alex over and over that I would be back playing hockey in no time at all. I must have said the same thing a lot, because I remembered the different answers they'd given me, the only things I was recalling in my fuzzy head. They didn't *mean* to change what they said each time, after all they were seeing the fact I wasn't recovering fast, and coming to their own conclusions. But they'd both stopped assuring me I would be back, and had begun offering alternatives. It was only through them that I knew how bad things were. When they began sentences with *you said that*, or, *we know*, then I realized I must have been repeating myself, and then I got to the point when I stopped talking at all. I wasn't surprised that they'd given up on me, and it didn't matter that they visited with their funny stories about the team, or about Alex falling in love, or Ryker getting engaged, I knew they didn't want to be there.

Why would anyone want to be there with me? I've never been the kind of guy anyone wanted as a friend, at least not for long, once they found out that I wasn't all laughter and sunshine, and that I was actually a mess of nerves and self-doubt. For a while Aarni had given me strength and a kind of protection from the world, but even that had gone horribly wrong.

"Henry? Are you in here?" Oscar called from the door, and I immediately pulled my knees up and crouched on the seat, the pain in my leg like a knife. He knocked on the cubicle door. "Are you okay? Do I need to call 911?"

Fuck his condescending tone of pity and exasperation. I didn't need anyone to call 911. I was a grown man perfectly capable of getting myself out of this bathroom and back home to my empty borrowed mansion.

You're just a kid, you think being twenty-four means that you have any handle on your life?

"I'm fine," I said with confidence.

"You're uhh… in the bathroom… doesn't seem like you're okay."

Fuck you Oscar! Leave me the hell alone. Go away.
"I'll be out in five."

Oscar let out a sigh. "You know this is for the best, the insurers will just find more loopholes and you'll end up with nothing."

I clambered down, the action taking a while as I unfolded my leg and had to breathe through the ache, and then holding myself up when I missed the handle and slammed headfirst into the door.

"Jesus, are you okay?"

I located the handle and unlocked the door, stepped out and past him, and to the basin where I carefully and methodically washed my hands. I felt unaccountably brave for a moment, and blurted out the question that gnawed away at me.

"What did Mom and Ed tell you?" I asked, without looking at him.

"Sorry?" He had that defensive edge to his voice, the one he'd used to explain how he had no idea what they'd done.

"I'm not stupid, a lawyer would have been involved in the kind of deals they made, so tell me again it wasn't you that was forging things?"

"I've already told you it wasn't me—"

"Oscar." I turned to face him. "I'm not signing the paperwork, you need to push the insurers for enough to clear everything I owe."

"Now, listen to me—"

"I will not spend the rest of my life paying back money that Ed and mom stole from me and handed out like candy."

"You signed the paperwork—"

"She handed it to me, what else was I going to do? Who am I paying back? Am I covering your debts as well?" I felt brave, strong, and god knows where it came from. "I'll need proof you knew nothing."

He took a menacing step toward me and I shrank back, my rush of confidence vanishing instantly.

"You little shit," he snapped.

The hand I could see clearly was curled into a fist and I braced myself for the hit. If I relaxed a little I could roll with the punch and it wouldn't hurt as much. I'd learned that from experience.

The door opened and two guys walked in, chatting about deeds and money and fuck knows what. I took the opportunity to slide past Oscar, trailing my hand along the wall so I could find my way without messing up. I knew he'd follow me. I'd seen the temper in him when he didn't get his own way. I headed to reception and out onto the street, turning right as best I could without my leg giving way, fighting the dizziness, and climbing into the first cab I saw. I gave the address to the huge place that Adler Lockhart had loaned to me, and only when I was inside the gates with the code engaged did I feel truly safe. At least I'd had the courage to confront Oscar, not that it had resulted in much and I certainly hadn't signed away my career for the little money I'd been offered. My vision was clouded, like a gray curtain moving over my eye, and I made it to the sofa before slumping into the corner. What did I do now? I was living in a borrowed place, with no access to money for specialists or support, and I was too ashamed to approach a team that was probably trying to find a way for me to leave.

It didn't matter that Coach Carmichael checked in on me three times a week at least, or that Ryker and Alex were all over me with their forced enthusiasm, I was alone here, and yet again it was too real for me. Tears leaked from my eyes, and the pressure in my chest grew until it was too much to contain. I sat in the huge empty front room with the high ceilings and sobbed until it hurt. Only when the crying jag was done and I felt even more pathetic than I had to start with, did I stumble to the bathroom to wash my face.

The mirror showed a man who had no backbone, a broken man, a *former* hockey player, someone who wasn't going to leave a mark on this world. *No wonder Aarni was so pissed at me. No wonder my mom and Ed took everything. I'm not surprised Oscar thinks I'm easy to lie to. I'm just a fucking waste of everyone's time.*

I stared at my reflection objectively, searching for my courage and somehow that became me checking for evidence of the injury that had destroyed my life. I understand the technical explanation of what had happened to me and had it written down, on the notes on my phone, and on repeat in my head in case I forgot. My retina had become separated from the nerve tissues and blood supply underneath it, it had detached, and the detached portion was no longer able to properly transmit light signals to my brain. Added to that, blood vessels were leaking fluid into the inner portion of the eye where there was usually a gel-like fluid. The experts said that I was lucky the retinal detachment hadn't progressed into the central part of the retina because then the impact on my vision could have been more severe.

More severe than the permanent cloud in my eye and the floating black spots?

"Lucky me," I said to my reflection.

My phone vibrated in my pocket and I pulled it out, tilting my head to read who was calling, seeing Adler's name. He was probably asking for his freaking house back. And why wouldn't he? This was prime Arizona real state, six bedrooms, seven bathrooms, a huge-ass kitchen, a pool, a gym. All that and I was *just* his friend's little brother. No one important. I ignored the call and put the phone back where it belonged.

I should have taken the money they offered, maybe kept at least some of it myself.

"Breathe. Just breathe. Everything will be okay." I was talking to my reflection again, and there was something so fucking stupid about this that I smiled to myself. "Talking to a mirror never ended well for the wicked queen," I murmured, and then left before my reflection could answer back.

Watching television got me another hour further through the day, some car program where they were rebuilding an old Plymouth Barracuda, which didn't hold my interest at all. When my phone vibrated again it was a welcome relief and unconsciously I needed to talk to someone right now. As long as it wasn't my mom, Oscar, or Adler.

Only it was Coach Carmichael.

My decision to answer was split-second. I owed the

man respect, so I connected the call, put it to loudspeaker, and dropped my cell in my lap.

"Hey, Coach." I would always call him that, even if I was on long-term injured reserve and wasn't actually part of the team for real.

"Hey, Henry. How are you doing?" he asked.

I bit back the instant response where I told him everything was shit. My vision wasn't getting better, the world was still blurry and I was tired. "Working hard," I lied. "Maintaining my fitness, working toward getting back to the team."

Coach paused then, and it was a pregnant pause full of a hundred awful things I could only imagine.

"That's why I'm calling you," he said.

My heart shattered at those words. This was it, the moment that the team said they couldn't wait any longer and that when my rookie contract was up I would be done with the Raptors. "Uh huh?" I said with as much confidence as I could muster, clearing my throat to ease the tension there.

"I wanted to be the one to tell you that management is concerned about…" the rest of what he said disappeared in a rush of white noise in my head. "Henry? Are you listening?"

"Yes," I lied.

"So when can we book the first session?"

What? "The first session?"

Now it was Coach's turn to clear his throat. "I was talking about Lorraine and when you can see her?"

"Who is Lorraine… sorry?"

"It's okay, son," Coach offered, and I wanted to cry

again for his soft, understanding tone. "Management have hired Lorraine Gaskell. She worked with Adam Sainz, remember him, goalie for Blues, shoulder surgery. Anyway, she's going to be working with you with a view to getting you back on the ice."

"Wait? She's a skater?" None of this was making sense.

"No, Henry," Coach was patient with me, "As I said, she's a sports psychologist, and an expert in her field dealing with sports injury and mental recovery."

"The team are… they're doing this?" *They're paying for this?*

"Henry, if there is a way to get you back on the ice, I want you there." Hope flared, and then extinguished as quickly when he continued talking. "And if she can't help, then I'm sure we'd find other options, if we have time."

I wanted to ask him what he meant, but voicing my question wasn't going to help me, because I knew where he was going with this. Too much time out of the game and my muscle memory would fade, my skills would soften, and then I'd be playing beer league on a Sunday.

He kept talking, "She wants you to go to her place for the first appointment, I'll book her and send you the time. I'm guessing there's no bad time?" He wasn't asking, he was telling, and that was exactly how I needed to be spoken to in order to push through the sticky syrup in my head.

Let me check my busy diary. "Whatever you think."

We ended the call with the normal pleasantries, but I felt as if I'd been run over by a steamroller. The Raptors were bringing in a psychologist for me? Hope that maybe the Raptors still wanted me was tempered with a subtle warning that time was running out, but I would take that glimmer of hope. With a burst of enthusiasm, I headed straight for the gym, stripped to my waist, and set a slow pace on the running machine, little more than a walk. Sweat poured down my face, dripping onto my chest, stinging my eyes. I'd lied about keeping up my fitness, but it wasn't for lack of trying, only walking was all I was managing right now, and I could feel the muscles I needed seizing up as I moved.

"Hola!" someone said and startled me so badly I stumbled back and collapsed in a heap on the floor, looking up at a blurry figure and knowing that there was no way I could run from whoever it was, even if I wanted to.

So I closed my eyes and rolled into a fetal position and waited for the hurt to start.

THREE

Apollo

THE GRIN SLID FROM MY FACE WHEN THE BIG MAN ON THE treadmill went to the floor then curled into a ball as if awaiting a kick in the head. I threw a confused look at my Tía Sofía standing in the doorway behind me. She towered over me, true, but the stunning woman in the svelte dress, hat, and heels wasn't *that* intimidating, even if she was six-foot-two. My aunt quirked a perfectly plucked black eyebrow.

Henry made a sound like a sick kitten. Something inside me took over before I could even think properly. I tugged the light shawl off my shoulders—the Lockhart jets were always chilly—and ran over to Henry lying on the floor.

"Oh my gosh, pudding, we're so sorry for sneaking up on you. Here, here now, sit up. It's all good. Yeah, that's right. Dang man, you went down hard. Are you okay?" I eased my arm under him, dropping to one knee then lifting him into a sitting position. He was clammy and stiff as a board. I draped my shawl around his shoulders, patting at his arms and such, checking to see if the tumble off the treadmill had broken anything. "You should always have the safety brake thing attached to your clothing."

Aunt Sofía walked to the treadmill, turning it off with a poke of a well-manicured finger. "Where's the kitchen? I'll fetch him a drink while the driver brings in your bags."

"Uhm I'm not sure, Tía. Adler didn't give me a floorplan, although maybe he should have."

"I'll find it. I have a nose for the second best room in the house," she countered, tapping her long, thin nose then sashaying off leaving me to tend to my new charge.

"Who are you?" Henry asked, his voice deep, soft, and shaky.

"I'm Apollo. Apollo Vasquez? Adler told me he'd informed your brother Dan that I was coming. No, sit here, my aunt Sofía will be back with a drink for you." I ran my hand over his back, rubbing softly in a circle right between his wide shoulders. He was quite a bit bigger than me, which wasn't unusual. I was small; strong, but small. "Do you feel funny? Did you hit your head? Ah see, here's Tía Sofía now. Here, take a sip. Easy. Good man."

His lips were pink, the lower one full. His gaze flickered from Sofía standing over him to me. I'd never seen such incredible eyes on a man. They were this beautiful light blue color, like a pale turquoise lake I'd seen once way up in Canada. He had graceful eyebrows, and thick lashes that framed his deeply sad eyes. His hair was short, wheat-gold, thick, and in need of a good wash and trim. Scars dotted his face, tiny ones that I assumed were from the tiny bits of glass from the shattered windshield. He looked Nordic, but his bearing was far from any Viking I'd ever seen on TV. Henry, for all his athletic bulk, reminded me of an abused kitten.

"Adler called me, a lot, but I... Does he want me out?" Henry asked after taking a few sips, his shaking hands quieting a bit.

"No, what? No, he wants you to stay here. That's why I came out." I sat beside him, gifted him my brightest smile, and patted his shoulder. "I'm here to be your companion until you're back on the ice."

He made a sound of dismissal. I had no clue what that was about, or anything really. I'd come into this half-blind and full of cheery optimism. This would be for the best. The warmth, the sun, the chance to feel needed again. Adler had told me little about Henry other than the barest facts I needed to know. He'd been in a car accident, had dated an abusive jerkoff, and was now trying to work his way back to playing.

"Can you stand, Mr. Greenaway?" Sofía asked, dropping down into a ladylike crouch beside me and tipping her head to the right. "Here, let me help you. Apollo, love, why don't you get behind us, in case Mr. Greenaway feels woozy."

With that, my aunt pulled Henry to his feet. I grabbed his biceps to steady him. He took a few steps, paused, handed me the water glass, and then slid out of the gym like a shadow wraith.

"Well, isn't he an unusual sort," she said.

"He's been through a lot. I'm going to go find him. I'm worried."

She patted my cheek with a big hand. "Of course you are. That's why we love you. Such a nurturing heart. Go, find your wounded wren. I'll go pick out a room for you. This place is lovely, by the way. Open and airy, filled with windows and breezeways. It will be perfect for you to give that SAD a boot in the ass."

I gave her a soft smile then jogged off to find Henry. The house was huge. Six bedrooms, seven baths, the Spanish décor spilled into the gardens and in-ground pool, which overlooked Tucson down below. Every room was spacious, open, with dark beams, arched windows, and glittering chandeliers. I wandered around for ten minutes until I stumbled across a door leading to a veranda. Henry was seated on a chaise with teal cushions. The grounds were sprawled out behind him, thick rows of red and pink flowers stretched to the base of the mountain that the mansion was situated under. An Olympic pool and a Spanish-motif pool house made a grand statement.

He looked just as my aunt had said, like a bird that had been mauled by a cat. My heart went out to him. I wanted to help him, heal him, hold his hand as he recovered from the emotional and physical pain he'd endured. Mostly, I wanted to see him smile. Just a little. I longed to see some life in those beautiful blue eyes of his.

"Hi," I called from the doorway, giving him plenty of warning that I was arriving. Lesson learned. Do not make a gay grand entrance unannounced. Pity, because I was so good at making those kind of entrances. "Are you feeling okay?"

The sun hit my face as I stepped out onto the smooth beige tiles. A warm wind ruffled the palms and played with the spider plants hanging from the stone archways. Oh my yes, this was paradise. I could feel the creepy tendrils of sadness lifting from me.

"Yeah, I'm fine. I just… you startled me." He ran a hand over the back of his neck, lifting his gaze from my bare feet. He was squinting. "Dan mentioned hiring someone. I didn't think it would be someone like you."

I crossed my arms over my little rainbow budgie tank top and popped a hip. "Are you upset over the fact that I'm so brightly queer or that I'm Latino?"

"*What?* No! I… what? I like Hispanic men, a lot. And women. People. I like people of Spanish decent. And men, I mean… I date men. Gay men. I like bright, gay men just fine. I just, I meant someone as pretty as you is all."

Oh. Oh. Oh shit. *Oh my.* "Sorry. I'm so sorry. I just assumed…" I waved a hand at myself, my skinny silver bangles jingling. "Sometimes jock types, even the gay ones, have trouble with a colorful, feminine man. Maybe we should start over. Hello, I'm Apollo Vasquez and I am *so* happy to be here! I hope we can become the best of friends."

I offered him my hand. He eyed it for a long moment, then slowly slid his much bigger one into mine. We shook, three times, and then he dropped it. He had a nice grip, firm, with long pale fingers.

"I'd like to be your friend too," he said, his cheeks pinking up. "I'm sorry for being so dense. Adler called me, a lot, but I just couldn't handle him so I let the calls go to voicemail."

"No worries. There are days no one can handle Adler,

his boyfriend included." I sat on a chair, the puffy teal cushion padding the wrought-iron frame nicely. I slung one bare leg over the other, reveling in the sunny love beams hitting my bare toes, calf, and thigh. I vowed I would wear nothing but shorts, tanks, and bare toes with tiny little toe rings the entire time I was here. "I am sorry over my jumping-to-conclusions rant. Truth be told I should have known that Adler wouldn't be friends with someone who wasn't accepting."

"I'm totally accepting."

"I know you are. That was my bad. How could anyone not like a beautiful queer like me bouncing into their home?" I threw my hands into the air. His eyes went round. Maybe I needed to tone down my fabulousness a little, it seemed to stun him. "Anyway, we're on new ground now. So, tell me, what would you like for dinner? I'm used to cooking for an athlete, so your meals will be high protein, lots of lean meats and veggies, dairy, carbs."

"Uhm, chicken. I like chicken. And cottage cheese."

"So do I," I replied, leaning back to let the rays shine on my face. "God, it is beautiful out here. I feel better already."

"Are you sick?"

I opened my eyes to find him staring at me. As soon as I saw him, he looked away. Why, I wondered? Maybe someday he'd not glance down when our eyes met.

"I've been down lately. I suffer from SAD, which is a seasonal disorder. Short days, lack of sun, cold weather, it all makes me very grumpy. I also had a bad relationship last summer, and I'm still not over it. That bad romance has made my winter blues worse." I sighed with passion, kicking my foot up and down. His gaze darted to my bouncy little foot. "He used me, told me lies, said he loved me but then he went out and fucked other guys behind my back." I had to shake off the memory of heading to Buffalo for a surprise birthday weekend to find him in bed with some slutty twink, my boyfriend's pasty white ass pistoning away as he plowed that skanky, skinny bitch of a waiter. "I mean, I flew up there to celebrate *his* fucking birthday. Thank the Virgin I didn't end up with some STD, as they were going at it bareback." I shuddered, my foot moving with more speed the angrier I got. "I'd been monogamous *as hell* while we were together. I loved that shitty assface."

"I'm sorry. My ex-boyfriend nearly killed me." His voice drifted off, as did his attention. "I loved his shitty assface too."

"Well aren't we a couple of big, fat failures in love?" Henry nodded. "Maybe this house will help heal us both. Let's try looking at the future through rose-colored glasses. We're entitled, right?"

"Sure, if you say so."

He was so timid for a hockey player. It was in direct contradiction to most of the Railers I knew. Timidity and ice hockey didn't really go together. It was an aggressive sport played by men who were generally assertive and hyper-masculine. I wondered what had made him so mousey and how I could help restore the grit he'd need for his return to the lineup.

"Ah, here you are! I'm thinking of leaving a trail of breadcrumbs the next time I leave the kitchen," Tía Sofía declared as she scurried out onto the veranda. "The driver has placed your bags in the room next to the blue bathroom with the gold fixtures. I have to go, dumpling. I need to get to the office and see if that order for Montreal went out. Give me a kiss."

She bent down. I dutifully pressed my lips to her soft cheek. Then she tapped her other cheek as Henry gawked at her. All the color he'd regained left his face as if someone had flushed a toilet. He was the shyest man I'd ever met. It was crazy appealing, as it was something that I'd not been exposed to much. There were lots of words to describe Apollo Vasquez, shy was not one of them. Still, for as many things we had that were different, we shared some vitally important things, broken hearts, and the need to find ourselves even though we faced an uncertain future.

"Such a blusher," Sofía teased, straightening as she slid on some dark shades. "Make sure you don't get lost, sweetie. We may never see you again."

"We'll never travel alone," I replied, getting a cheeky snort from my aunt. She swayed off, her long legs carrying her out of view in just a few strides. I turned my head in time to catch Henry staring at the rounded doorway. "She's some kind of impressive, huh?"

"I've never seen a woman as tall as she is," he confessed.

"All the tall genes in the family went to her. So, want to go find the kitchen? I hate airplane food so I skipped eating. My stomach is back on east coast time." I slid my hand up under my top to rub my stomach. Henry watched with interest, his cheeks growing red when I gave him a wink. "You hungry?"

"A little." He stood and walked off. Either I made him really nervous or that was a tic of his. I'd have to dig a bit to see if it was some quirk that had shown up after the accident, or if he'd always been prone to being so socially awkward. Head injuries were terrible things, all of us who called Tennant Rowe-Madsen friend knew that firsthand. I shot to my feet to race after him, fearful of getting lost in this huge-ass mansion and never being heard from again.

———

TWO DAYS LATER, I WAS EMPTYING THE LAST OF MY BOXES that had arrived from Harrisburg via the moving service. I'd dithered for over ten days, mulling and fretting, until finally reaching my decision to fly out and help Henry. Adler had never pushed me one way or the other, mostly because he wasn't home. The Railers were gearing up for the playoffs which would start in about three weeks. Between the traveling and the nights at Layton's... well, he wasn't there to nudge. So, in the end, I opted to send out about two-thirds of my personal belongings. Now I was glad I had.

My bedroom was richly appointed in dark golds and browns, the doors and closets were thick, heavy wood fashioned in the old-time Spanish décor that ran throughout the manse. The windows were wide open, the desert winds sweeping down the side of the Santa Catalina mountains, blowing the sheers up and out like gauzy wraiths hobbled yet intent on freeing themselves.

My clothes were all unpacked, hung up or folded and placed into the massive dressers, and I'd placed my family photos all around. Now I just had to hang the cross that had been handed down to me from my many times great-grandmother from Santiago de Cuba. Balancing on the bed because Jesus had to look down on you while you were sleeping, I took down the painting of a pink and purple desert as "Justify My Love" was blaring out of my phone resting in its little docking unit/speaker thing.

"*Hola!*"

I squeaked in fright, spinning around and clutching the painting to my chest to find Henry in the open doorway, dressed in running shorts and a Raptors T-shirt, a quirky kind of amused look playing on his lips.

"My God and the blessed Mary, you scared the shit out of me!" I panted, easing the painting to the bed so that I could pat my thumping heart with my hand. "Do you need anything?"

"We have to leave for the doctor and physical therapy." He lingered in the doorway as if scared to enter, his hair damp from his shower. I thought to ask why shower before PT but I didn't, because who was I to question?

"Yeah, at two this afternoon. It's only nine in the morning," I gently pointed out. I was learning that Henry disliked being late for any reason. "Come in and help me unpack then we can go for a walk around the grounds." He eased into the room one timid step at a time. "Good, now hand me that big cross there in that box on the dresser." I waved in the general direction. "Yep, that's it."

"It's heavy." He carried it over to me. I thanked him then spun, letting him enjoy the view of my ass in a pair of pink knit jean shorts. He'd look. He was gay. He'd have to give me a peek.

"Right? It's super old. It belonged to my great-great-great-great-grandmother."

"Wow."

"Yeah, she brought it with her when she and her sister immigrated from Cuba back in 1897." I had no clue as to what kind of wood it was crafted from, but it was walnut-toned. The figure of Jesus was worn smooth from so many generations of fingers touching his toes. As soon as it was on the nail, I did just that, touched his toes then crossed myself. I wasn't a huge church-goer for some obvious reasons, but one didn't grow up in a Latino household and not touch Jesus' toes then make the sign of the cross. My grandmother would've slapped us goofy if we'd passed the cross without paying the proper homage.

"So, you're Cuban."

I fiddled with the cross to get it straight then turned to peek down at Henry.

"Partly." I handed the painting to him then turned to study the cross. It was crooked, so I adjusted it, taking a few steps back to make sure it was straight. My heel slid off the edge of the mattress. Arms pinwheeling, I shouted in fright and tumbled backwards off the bed like a drunken hippo. Henry caught me with a grunt, my back slamming into his chest. When my feet hit the floor I spun around too quickly, our chests rubbing deliciously. I pawed at him, getting a finger into the neck of his T-shirt. He jerked away, flinging my hand aside, which threw me off-balance. I grabbed at his arm, fingers biting into thick biceps, to right myself. Henry skittered in reverse, his arm still in my grip, as I made several apologies. I'd come to understand that the man didn't like to be touched unexpectedly. "Sorry, sorry. I'm so clumsy at times."

I released his arm, moved away, and carried the painting to the massive walk-in closet beside one of four big, arched windows. "It's okay," I heard him say as I slid the painting behind my clothes, embarrassment heating my cheeks. Taking a second to calm myself from that chest-on-chest friction, I sauntered out of the closet a moment later and found him checking out the pictures on my dresser. "Is this you?"

I padded over on bare feet then smiled at the framed photo in his hand. "No, that's Mama and Tía Sofía, and the old man with them was my paternal grandfather. This was taken in Luquillo, where my father's family was from."

"Is that in Mexico?" he asked, his attention riveted to the two children of six or seven in the picture. "My friend Alex is Mexican-American."

"No, Puerto Rico. I'm a mixed bag of fabulous Latino heritage." He gave me a timid smile, just a twitch of the corner of his mouth, but oh my stars it made my heart skip several beats. "This," I lifted the picture of my father in his uniform from beside my bangle box, "is my father, Manolito Vasquez. Him, his sister, and his parents moved from Puerto Rico to Maine where my grandmother's brother owned a successful accounting firm. Papa didn't like numbers, so instead of going into the firm as his family expected him to, he joined the Army. This was taken the day he enlisted at twenty. He and Mama had been married for a year then. She'd gotten pregnant but lost my brother after a hurried wedding. He went to Afghanistan before I was born and died over there when his transport was hit by an IED. I was born two months after he was buried."

"That sucks," he said. I nodded. "You never got to meet him?"

"No, but Mama talks about him all the time, so I feel like I know him. He was a hero."

"Yeah, he was." He studied Papa deeply. "He's handsome. You take after him."

"Thank you. I think you're handsome too." The tips of his ears went beet red. I placed Papa's picture back then leaned in closer to peek at the photograph Henry still held. "I don't get to see my family in Cuba or Puerto Rico much. I'm proud to be Latino but I'm so Americanized my Cuban relatives laugh at me when we do speak."

"Why is your aunt dressed like a boy?" he asked as I knew he would.

"Because she *was* a boy." I let that dangle so he could soak it up at his own speed. I watched the wheels clicking and spinning as he put two and two together. When his gaze flew from the photo to me, I waggled a freshly tweezed eyebrow.

"Oh, wow, I never would have…"

"She's my hero too, her and Papa and Mama. My family is packed full of people to admire."

"I wish mine was." He placed the photograph back and eased around me, slipping out of the door to be by himself for a spell.

I thought to follow him but sensed he needed to regroup. He seemed to be unable to interact for long stretches, as if his socializing well ran dry quickly. I'd give him space, then around lunch time go find him. He'd either be in the gym, in the pool, out among the flowers, or seated on the veranda with his nose in a book. By then he'd be fine and willing to talk a bit before he withdrew again. I was figuring out that life with Henry was all about balance.

Guess I needed to work on my dismounts.

FOUR

Henry

PT WAS HELL ON EARTH, AND I DIDN'T CARE WHO KNEW how I felt about it.

So much of my life, from the moment I'd taken my first step, was about balance. I didn't remember my first skate on the ice. Dan had told me I was eighteen months old, and that I was wearing sneakers, copying him as he tested out his first ever skates. The way he told it, I was a natural, only I ended face down in a snow drift, and he'd said I cried for most of the day.

I do recall my first skates, the ones passed down to me from Dan, and I knew I fell on my butt. Maybe it was just twice my first time on them, or ten times, and maybe the next week I skated off the edge of the pond and into a bush, or pinwheeled straight into the tiny broken jetty. All I did recall was that the most important thing in skating was staying upright by understanding the physics of my own body.

Of course, there was also the added confidence things; twenty miles an hour on sharp blades, running into walls, getting pushed and shoved, fighting for a disc so small that sometimes it was lost in the snow around the pond hockey. And then there was skill. I couldn't be a hockey player without skill, some of which was learned muscle memory, and some of which was instinct, or maybe just the way I was built. I had strong legs, and I was fast.

I was fast.

I may have been quiet, and I'd never be a leader in the room, but I got the job done. Somehow in all those tumbles and missteps, I found a way to skate and play and balance my speed with my skill, but somehow now I couldn't even stand properly without falling over.

"Okay, I need you up on your toes," my torturer instructed. She had the whitest blonde hair I'd ever seen, braided and pinned ruthlessly so it was flat against her head, and her hazel eyes held no affection when she worked with me. Her name was Millie, and she had a wonderful life with a husband and two kids, and a house in the burbs. I knew because when she'd finished worsening my pain levels she changed from strict and no-nonsense to proud momma with photos on her phone. I could've hated her for what she made me do in PT, but I felt stronger each time we were done.

Apart from my legs feeling like jelly, that was.

"And relax," Millie said.

I gently stood flat on the floor again, my hands flexing on the poles.

"Again, but this time let go of the poles."

What? I couldn't balance without them. What about my eye injury? Didn't she realize that I was struggling with the one thing I had taken for granted?

"I can't," I began but she just ignored me. "I need to—"

"Let go of the bars, Henry, up on your toes, in three, two…"

I huffed as I went up on my toes, and let go of the wood, my fingers hovering an inch above, ready to grab it when I wobbled, and wobble I did. I gripped the bars, and came back to a stand.

"Henry—"

"What do you want me to do!"

"Not rely on the wood," she explained with exaggerated patience. "Choose a new point of focus that relies on your good eye, and keep upright on your own."

"It's not easy when I can't find that center of focus." I sounded like a hopeless kid, but I wasn't lying. All my life I'd had two good eyes to rely on, and now my right eye was fucked up and useless. I'd lost the peripheral vision, and who knew if I would ever get that back, then there were the floaters that clouded my vision. Why didn't she understand that this wasn't helping?

"Again," she repeated.

With a noisy sigh of disbelief I did as I was told, hands on the bars, up on my toes, my calf muscles tensing in protest after a few seconds, and releasing my hands enough to come up and off the wood. I wobbled again, grabbed the bars, and cursed under my breath. I was messing this up big time, and worst of all, Apollo was on a chair in the corner of the gym watching me. For two weeks I'd tried to avoid him in the house, and for two weeks he'd followed me around like a puppy. I went to the gym and he sat on a bench. I was in my room, he would knock on the door and demand we go for a walk in the grounds. I came back from the walk and he fed me. He was there all the freaking time and it was driving me mad, because he never said a bad word to me so I couldn't be angry with him. He never once told me that I was doing something wrong. Instead, he gently encouraged me to think about what I was doing so I came to my own conclusion that I was fucking up. I wasn't walking far enough. I wasn't eating enough food. I spent too much time wallowing.

But these were all my words, not his. He encouraged me to walk a little farther each time to see a special flower or bush he'd found. He made food so nice that I was encouraged to eat. As to the wallowing, he would hover, then sit with me, and turn on the television, or read a book. Anything so I stopped concentrating on whatever shit was messy and scrambled in my head.

The guy was so damn nice, and I had a hard time finding something to dislike about him, and that just made me more determined, because clearly the car accident had made me an idiot.

"Concentrate please," Millie snapped and pulled me from my rambling thoughts. "Let's try this a different way." She tapped the bar, and I sent her a grateful half smile that she wouldn't make me do something I couldn't ever hope to do, but my smile was premature. "Hands back on the bars."

"Huh?"

"Hands on the bars, up on tiptoes, and close your eyes."

"Close my eyes?"

"Yes, I want you to hold the position for ten, and then relax."

"Wait, what? With my eyes shut?"

"Three, two…"

Anger spiked inside me, but I pushed it away to do what I'd been told, then moved to tiptoes, settled my breathing and let go of the handrail as I closed my eyes. For one exhilarating moment my body did exactly what it was supposed to do and the elation was so intense it overwhelmed me, until in the space of a millisecond I lost my balance and fell sideways, yelping as my hip contacted the bar.

"You're okay," Millie reassured, "again."

I rubbed at my sore hip, feeling an unaccountable desire to cry, which was not on a hockey player's to-do list. Not that I *was* a hockey player at the moment. I wanted to be, but what team would take a chance on a visually impaired player whose backstory was one of weakness and shame? What Coach Carmichael saw in me I didn't know.

I want to go back, I'll work hard. That was what the angel on one shoulder promised me. The devil though, he was sitting there cackling in my ear about how shit I was, what a failure I was, and mostly how all of this was my fault. I shouldn't have gotten into the car with Aarni, even if concern for his state of mind had me worrying he'd do something stupid. I shouldn't have let myself back down after I told him to stop the car and he ignored me.

Instead of giving into either, I shoved them aside and closed myself off. Things were easier that way.

By the time I left PT, heading for the new head doctor,

I was grumpy, sad, quiet, and Apollo was chattering away about nothing and it was getting on my last nerve.

"… so then my cousin, you remember the one who did the thing with the jam? Well, he just told everyone it was me that drew on the wall with the lipstick, even though it was so not my color, and then it hit the fan. Literally. I threw the glitter at him, it hit his head, went up into the fan and the shiny stuff rained everywhere. I swear it ended up in every crevice on me and the house. So Julio, that's my cousin by marriage who lives in Havana, the one with the hair that will not be tamed, he makes it even worse by bringing glue to the heated debate. I mean, who brings glue into a glitter situation?" He paused and I think he wanted me to answer, or at least let out a generic hmmm noise, but my hip ached, my head hurt, my vision was blurry, and I was fucking done. A great well of misery and self-loathing spat out of me in a vomit of words

"I don't know your family, and I don't fucking care," I snapped, and then instantly realized what I'd done. This wasn't me. I didn't lose my cool with people, I didn't upset strangers, let alone the man who made the best chili I'd ever tasted. *What am I doing?* "Shit. Shit. Stop the car. Please stop the car."

Apollo pulled into a side road immediately, blinkers on, and turned to face me, but I was up and out of that car so fast that it made my head spin. Blackness consumed me, my lungs stopped processing air, I was dying on the sidewalk in front of god knows where, and not only that but Apollo was going to be furious with me. He'd leave me, then Adler would find out and give up on me, Dan would be pissed I'd fucked this chance up, and I would be finished.

No hockey. No life. No money. Nothing.

I can't breathe, I can't...

I grabbed the nearest thing to me, some kind of fence post, and leaned there, terrified when I couldn't get air in my lungs, and then something broke through, the theme tune to some kids show, Apollo's singing soft in my ear, and his hands on me, holding me up.

I leaned into his hold, realizing that I might squash him, and centering my balance just a little so I didn't hurt him. Slowly my breathing came under my control, and the theme to one of my favorite kids shows about a bear now played in my brain instead.

"Hey," Apollo said in his softest tone. "Do you need me to segue into the Goddess that is Madonna herself? I can do that, you know." He began to hum a familiar tune, and I recognized a hummed version of "Live to Tell", and memories of when I was little and Mom was still *Mom*, flooded back to me. *Before dad died. Before Ed.* They were worse than recalling the bear show. "There, your breathing is better," Apollo murmured.

Then somehow I was back in the car. I blinked and checked around me, expecting a crowd of people with phones capturing the entire embarrassing breakdown, but the road we'd parked on wasn't residential, just home to an outlet store that had been closed down.

"I'm sorry," I said.

"What for?" Apollo quirked a smile. "For being tired, and emotional, and for telling me that I was talking too much about things that aren't important to you?"

"They are. Important I mean, everything about you is important to me." I colored then and stared at my hands in my lap. "I didn't mean that *you* are important to me." *God, I'm making this worse.* "But you are, I mean not in any way that…" I sighed noisily because I was making no sense at all. "I don't snap at people like that."

Apollo patted my knee, and I winced automatically waiting for him to tell me it was all going to be okay. Instead, he focused on what we should *actually* have been doing.

"You ready to get to Doctor Gaskell?"

"Don't you want to talk about what just happened?" I waited for him to laugh at my stupid question, or maybe comment on what happened. But he stared at me and his gorgeous eyes didn't contain anything like censure or pity.

"Do *you* want to talk about it?" he asked.

"No."

Apollo started the car and pulled out into traffic. "I wonder what the doctor will be like?" he mused as he glanced at the navigation and indicated to pull onto the freeway. Lorraine Gaskell's clinic was fifteen miles outside of Tucson. I didn't answer, too lost in my own thoughts, and before I knew it, Apollo had turned on the stereo and thumbed to a playlist that showed up as Madonna, singing along with random hits as we headed south.

The building that housed the LG Sports Therapy clinic was set back from the main road, right at the end of a long driveway, and it seemed as if it was a converted home instead of a purpose-built space. There was a large oak front door, windows sparkling in the sunlight, and the garden was just as immaculate as the one at Adler's mansion. There was money here, but if Lorraine was as good as the reviews I'd read implied, then there was a reason for the sudden flare of hope in my chest.

"Do you want me to come in with you?" Apollo asked, indicating the book in the cubby between our seats. "Happy to find a shady corner and read if not."

Was it wrong to feel bereft at the thought of Apollo not coming in with me? "Why this time?"

"Hmm?" Apollo looked up from the cubby and smiled at me in that way he had when he didn't quite understand. It was a smile I'd seen a few times, a hesitant but warm expression of his interest in what I had to say. Bit by bit that smile was wearing me down.

"You never ask me if I want you to go into PT with me, so why ask me now?"

Apollo patted my knee, the warmth of his hand on my bare skin reassuring. "I know you now," he said, as if that explained everything.

You don't know me at all. No one knows me.

"It's okay for you to come in." I attempted to keep all traces of hope out of my voice, annoyed that I had somehow begun to rely on Apollo more than I truly needed to. The last time I'd let myself need someone had been Aarni. He'd become too much a part of me, the only person I'd needed, to the exclusion of others, and my *normal* therapist, the one dealing with my fucked up brain, had said that I shouldn't allow myself to *need* too much. Was I doing that right now with Apollo? "I don't need you," I added after a pause, "but the AC will be on inside."

Apollo's sweet smile faltered a little, but I had to cling

to the fact that this wasn't on me. I was just doing what my therapist had told me by taking some ownership of myself and believing that I was enough on my own. Of course, she'd said way more than that, but it was the one thing I clung to and used to excuse my past stupidity with men like Aarni. I didn't mean to make Apollo's smile slip, but I didn't have the emotional capacity to talk my way around what I'd said.

We headed inside, the floors marble, a large chandelier above our heads, and the cool peace and silence was exactly what my overheated brain needed.

"Oh goodness," a voice came from behind us, and I moved slowly to face a woman who crossed the marble, her hand extended to shake. "Henry Greenaway, I'm such a fan, I remember that wraparound in the final game of last season against Buffalo. You took that pass from Madsen, and you skated so fast I thought you wouldn't stop in time, and then you bypassed two defenders, and still managed to get around the back of the net and take LeMarque by surprise. The look he gave you, and the curses, what a win."

Great. She's a Raptors fan, wanting to relive past glory. Is that really the kind of therapy I need? Still, I recalled that goal, and it was one of my finer moments.

"Thank you, ma'am."

"Anyway, enough of that, and you are?" She extended her hand to Apollo, and I realized I'd ignored introductions.

"This is Apollo—"

"Apollo Vasquez—"

We talked over each other, but Apollo deferred to me,

and that was where I fucked things up, because I wanted to call him my friend but he wasn't that really. He was a paid companion, the guy who cooked, and made me walk places, and then checked on me when I was in bed.

"He's my—"

"A friend of Henry's," Apollo finished smoothly.

She smiled. "Couples therapy is always a useful part of the process, and bringing a partner is a good step in the right direction."

Partner? I stared at her stupidly.

"I'm not, we're not—"

"I'm more of an administrator," Apollo slid in smoothly. "Here to support Henry on his journey to getting back on the team."

Lorraine didn't miss a beat. "This way, please."

We followed her through a large empty gym filled with the most up-to-date machines I'd ever seen outside the Raptors' gym, and down a short corridor to an area that was more like someone's lounge than a waiting room. Deep, plush sofas formed separate areas, and there was a full-on coffee machine, next to a simpler pod coffee maker, along with a hundred different color pods.

"We'll get a drink and head on in," she said, and then gestured to the sofas. "Apollo, please make yourself at home, bathrooms are back the way we came, and just to go through fire safety, if the alarm sounds then the exits are marked clearly. Now, that is out of the way, who would like coffee? I can only do the pods, my husband is the user of big-Silver here, but he's not around today."

We selected pods, she made the coffees, then Apollo took a seat, and Lorraine and I went into another room.

Just like the waiting area, this was less office and more sofa heaven. She waited for me to choose a seat before sitting in one opposite, curling her legs up under her. I tried to relax but the stress was building with the whole not knowing what she was going to say.

"Do you know what I do?" she finally asked.

"I read up on sports psychology, and I have a couple of friends who have been through it, so yes, I have a general idea."

She laughed then, "I deal with body and mind, I'll put both through their paces, work on getting you back on the ice. Athletes are often left with mental scars long after an injury is physically healed, and I know you are still having issues with your eyesight, is that right?"

"Yeah, my eye," I said and touched a hand to my temple as if my description hadn't made it perfectly clear.

"Okay, well in basic terms, I'll talk you through the pressures associated with returning to your prior level of performance—pre-injury, work through the quality and efficiency of practice, and develop mental skills used during any of your pregame routines. We'll work on fears you may have, of failure, or future injury, and anything else that might be mentally blocking you. I'll liaise, with your permission, with your eye specialist, then we'll get you back on the ice, and the team. Does this all make sense to you?"

"Yes. But, do you really think I can—?"

"In addition, I ask for three things in a client-therapist relationship: honesty, hard work, and trust. You trust I am giving you the best advice, and I trust that you are doing your best with what I give you. I'll need one hundred percent transparency from you, and this will form our counseling sessions, and the hard work won't just be mental, but also on physical endurance. We have three months to get you to Raptors training camp and this won't be an easy road, but I need to ask you one thing, Henry Greenaway." She paused, and I wondered if it was just for effect or did she need me to say something there? However, before I could say a word, she placed her coffee on the small table between us and looked me right in the eye.

"Do you want to play hockey again?"

That was easy to answer. It was all I wanted to do. "Yes."

"Will you work hard?"

I recalled the half-hearted nonsense I'd been doing in recovery, and knew I'd already lost so much conditioning. I'd need to work more than hard to get back to status quo, and if she thought I could get back on the ice, if the Raptors still wanted me, then I could work so damn hard she'd be amazed by my dedication. "Yes."

Yes, as long as you don't make me stand there with my eyes closed.

"Okay then, next up, will you always tell me the truth even if you think I don't want to hear it?"

Fuck. "Yes."

She settled back in her seat looking a hundred kinds of innocent, and then she rocked my entire world.

"So, shall we start with an easy question?"

"Okay." *I can do this.*

"Tell me about your relationship with Aarni Lankinen."

FIVE

Apollo

MARCH MELTED AWAY INTO APRIL AND HENRY WAS STILL on long-term injured reserve. It wasn't any kind of surprise of course, we both knew he was in no way ready for playing hockey, but I could see it hurt him. He was a quiet man, prone to thoughtfulness and long stretches of silence that I simply was not used to, not yet anyway. Growing up with Adler Lockhart meant that I was accustomed to steady talking. Most of it silly nonsense such as if Batman and Captain America were lovers who would be the top, or were flying ants winging away from wingless uncles, or if you crossed a zebra with a turtle would you end up with a zurtle.

There was always noise, or had been for years, and the quietude was part of the reason that I'd felt so lost back in Harrisburg. Now I was facing the same silent hours and it was pulling down on me, making me feel sad. So I upped my sun box time and decided that this big old mansion needed some life hauled into it. Being so isolated couldn't be good for Henry, and I knew it was making me morose, so it was time to fix that.

The night of the Raptors' last regular season game against San Jose, Henry and I were in the airy living room, the evening breeze ruffling the sheers on the open bay doors. He was seated on a long sofa when I entered with a platter of cottage cheese and pineapple in sundae glasses. The man did have a healthy love of dairy products, I'd learned.

"You okay watching the game?" I inquired as I passed along our evening treat. He nodded, taking the sundae dish and long spoon with a soft little murmur of thanks. I nodded, tucking my left leg under my ass as I sat, and began spooning curds and fruit into my mouth as the game started. "You'll be out there on the ice come September."

"Yeah, I want to be but this eye…"

I glanced his way, my spoon resting on my lower lip for a moment. "You'll learn how to work around it, I promise. I've been reading up on hockey players with eye injuries, and lots of them bounce back after rehab. They'll teach you how to work around the losses that might linger."

His light blue eyes flickered to me. "How are you always so upbeat?"

I sniggered a little, waving my empty spoon around as the Raptors were whistled down for an offside.

"I have a magic box that has the sun inside it," I replied, giving him a cock-eyed smile that he reciprocated. Seeing him smile, a real honest smile, did funny things to my insides. Things that felt like joy and relief and friendship and… attraction.

"Can I borrow your magic box when I feel down?"

"Any time. Just come to my room and you'll feel better in no time," I tossed out glibly, hoping to ignore the burbling feelings taking place inside me. When his eyebrows darted up his forehead, I stammered and shifted uncomfortably. "That wasn't at all what I meant," I said awkwardly. "I meant you can borrow my sun box to make you feel better, not that *I* could make you feel better in my bed. Which I could, sure, because I'm pretty fabulous in bed! No, I'm not. Well, yes, I am, or so people tell me, but… this whole conversation is naughty. Eyes on the puck, Greenaway!"

I shoved a spoonful of cottage cheese into my mouth, my face hot.

Henry laughed softly, his spoon hitting the sides of the sundae dish as he fished around for a chunk of chopped pineapple. "I believe you."

I peeked to the side while San Jose blew through the Raptors defense to take a shot on goal. Colorado kicked it away with ease, and the second line picked up the puck and skated down to try their luck on the San Jose tender. I cocked an eyebrow at the man.

"I believe that you're fabulous in bed. You're pretty fabulous everywhere else."

Oh, holy shitballs. My balls grew hot and heavy, and my dick, which had been uninterested in anything sexual since seeing my ex fucking the stars out of someone else, stirred.

"I uhm… we should have a party for the team, to celebrate!" I threw out in a lame attempt to get things back on track. A clean track. The track that ran through You're-

His-Friend-and-Companion-so-Stop-Getting-Hard-Stupid-Dick-Ville.

"Celebrate what? Not making the playoffs?" he asked, his pale cheeks flushed and pink as posies. God, he was pretty in a classic Nordic way. A shy, injured Viking sorely in need of soft arms and a tender heart like mine too—

I dropped my spoon to my lap, eyes wide, body lighting up like a Christmas tree. "I uhm, yes! No, well, not really but celebrating that you guys came in fourth and not seventh! I'll go plan it now. In my room. With the door shut. After a shower." I stood and the spoon clattered to the hardwood floor.

"You took a shower after our walk this evening," he pointed out just as the Raptors defense broke down in front of Colorado, giving San Jose far too much time to pepper the goalie with rocket-like shots that bounced off Penn's chest, leg pads, and blocker. One eventually rolled into the corner and was picked up by Ryker Madsen who was then crushed into the boards. The puck squibbed free of our young guns. Alex was unable to corral it, then was cross-checked, the penalty unseen by the refs. All manner of shit then broke out in the corner, shoving, face washing with stinky gloves, and a punch thrown by Colorado at the San Jose forward closest to him. The fight that broke out then was pretty epic and took Henry's attention from me and my just-washed self.

I snuck off as he yelled at the refs about goaltender interference, even though Penn had been the one to punch an opposing player in the back of the head. Once in my room, I leaned on my bedroom door, sundae dish in hand, and prayed to old wooden Jesus that I wasn't allowing myself to fall for another man whom I thought I could save by virtue of my love. My therapist back in Harrisburg had warned me about loving broken men yet here I was, falling for a very broken, hurting man. Ugh, it was seven-year-old me and the bunny the gardener had hit with the weed eater all over again…

Only Henry wasn't a bloody cottontail, he was a man who thought I was fabulous and had sad, stunning eyes and an ass just begging to be—

My eyes flew to Jesus.

"Don't you pay no mind to my thoughts. Only listen to the spoken words, okay?"

He didn't reply. I ran into the shower, cranked the taps to cold, stripped, shrieked into a loofah sponge when the icy water hit my belly, and danced in circles until my balls were hiding inside my body and all thoughts of doing sexy things with Henry's bubble butt had been temporarily washed away.

A WEEK LATER I WAS ELBOW-DEEP IN FOOD PREP WITH MY aunt directing the madness.

"Why are we having chili?" Tía Sofía asked, lifting the lid on one of twenty or so crockpots before dipping a chunk of bread stolen from a platter for fondues into the spicy, bean-heavy dish. "I thought this was a fondue party."

"It is, but Henry likes chili and cottage cheese," I threw out as I dropped cubed pimento cheese into one of the pots bubbling away on the veranda.

"Is there anything that lad doesn't like cottage cheese

on or with?" She popped her bite into her mouth, made a yummy sound, and then dashed around the big table to grab a bottle of water from a tub filled with water, soda, and non-alcoholic beer. "*Santo Dios*," she huffed while fanning her face. "That's amazing. I can't feel my tongue."

"So it doesn't need more jalapeño then?" I asked as Henry ambled out of the mansion, his gaze flitting over the pots and balloons, all in the Raptors gold and brown and red color scheme. "How was your nap?"

"Good. Is that your chili?" He smiled at my aunt who was now dabbing her tongue with an ice cube. "Looks like it's four-alarm just the way we like it."

We. The way *we* liked it. I bit down on a reply that would have been sappy, I was sure. I liked the way *we* sounded coming from him, though, good intentions be damned. I wanted to be part of a we again. Being the second half of a *we* was my happy place. I missed having someone to fuss over as only a lover can fuss. My arms ached to hold a man, my hands yearned to touch, and my heart pined to be loved.

"… you're not Latino?" Tía Sofía was saying when I jerked back to the present. Henry laughed in that funny, snorty way of his. The edge of the knife slid over my fingernail, the miss a near one. Eyes on the blocks of cheese and not the man I was being paid to take care of, I cubed like a maniac as Henry stood there in shorts, sandals, and a tank top that showed off the definition he was slowly getting back into. Tía Sofía was wearing a summery dress with white heels, her black hair falling in thick waves over bared shoulders. I'd gone with something bright and festive. A red floral romper with bright yellow dahlias that buttoned down the front, paired with banana-toned one strap sandals. I'd loaded up on bangles and anklets as well, because it was a party after all.

"I'm pretty sure I'm not even a little Latino," he answered as he neared the chili pot like a thief sneaking up on a jewelry store. I waved my cheesy knife at him and got a flash of white teeth in a smile that nearly rocked me right off the veranda. "Although my grandmother visited Mexico on a bus tour once, so maybe?"

Tía Sofía sniggered around the ice cube she was now sucking on. "Then you probably are. I bet your grandma was wooed and wooed properly on her vacation. Who can resist a Latino man?" Henry's gaze met mine over the blue cheese fondue pot. My pulse jumped. He wet his lower lip. "Oh! That's the doorbell. My job as official greeter of hot, young hockey players begins!"

Off she ran, leaving Henry and me gaping at each other like dimwitted goldfish. The moon was just coming up over the mountains, Madonna's "La Isla Bonita" played on the home stereo system, and a gentle wind carried the cricket song to us. It was a long, poignant moment, one that could have easily seen me leaning over the artichoke and spinach fondue pot to press my needy lips to his. I think he would have let me, his eyes were hooded and filled with a million things I couldn't read, but then Tía Sofía arrived with Colorado Penn and his entourage. Rockers, groupies of both sexes all in skimpy swim gear, and an emu that ran over and started eating the bread cubes. A scuffle broke out between the emu and me. I lost. The big bird darted down the steps to the grounds with four girls in bikinis in hot pursuit, his beak full of pilfered bread.

"An emu? Really?" I asked Colorado as I dumped the emu-pecked bread that remained into the trash can under the table and pulled out a new loaf to hack up into bite-sized squares.

"He came with Lizzy, or was it Tommy?" He shrugged. "His name is Kricker the Flightless Lord of Ozone. Totally kickass bird. We're thinking of taking him on tour with us this summer," Penn replied, tossing his long dark hair from his face then hugging Henry close. For a long, long time. Too long. I gripped the knife a little tighter and cut bread with more vigor. "You guys have to come see us sometime. We're doing a west coast swing all the way up to Oregon."

"Henry doesn't really like to be touched," I snapped.

Tía Sofía gave me an odd look. Penn laughed, kissed Henry on the cheek, and then led him off to hang out with his slutty groupie guys who really should've worn more clothes or had smaller packages crammed into their Speedos. Soon, people had engulfed Henry. Touchy people. I cut cubes furiously, my aunt's dark eyes locked on me until the bell rang, calling her back into duty. It was nine o'clock. People started filing in, players and spouses filled the veranda, children had been left at home as per my request. I'd not wanted Henry to be upset by screaming kids. Not that I had any chance to worry over him as I'd not seen him since Colorado had led him away.

"Apollo, dude, stop cutting up bread cubes and join us," Ryker called over the music rolling out into the warm night. Music that wasn't Madonna at all. I suspected

Colorado had monkeyed with the whole house stereo somehow. I know for a fact that I did *not* have any Avenged Sevenfold on any of my playlists. I knew because I had had to ask Jacob, Ryker's fiancé, who the hell the band playing was.

I waved him off, too cranky to socialize. Tía Sofía was seated on a divan, blowing bubbles as Penn's groupies danced about to the screaming guitars. Where Colorado was I had no clue but I had plenty of suspicions. The manse was nothing but bedrooms. Ryker strode over, took the bread knife from me, and pulled me into the party-goers. I sulked, arms folded, my gaze moving over the team looking for Henry and not finding him. Ryker huffed then took me by the arm, leading me through the throngs to introduce me to all the players. I met Alex and his British boyfriend. Then I met the towering Russian captain Vlad Novikov. I met players of every name and nationality and their lovely wives, or boyfriends if they mowed my side of the lawn.

"… hear about the buzz coming in Dallas?" Vlad asked the small group I had been pulled into. His English was quite good, much better than Stan's. "I'm picking up small items on the internet about Tate Collins and the woman he was to marry. Details are sketchy but she's on this reality show, and there are whispers that she has attacked another woman online, pulling him into the mess somehow."

"No shit," Ryker said as he nursed a beer. "What did she say to this other woman?"

Vlad shrugged a huge shoulder just once. He reminded me of that big Russian in that one Rocky movie. "It's not clear yet."

"Maybe it's a jealousy thing. Like Tate was playing around with two women at once," Alex offered, his arm resting around Sebastian's waist. "I've never seen a player with more women than Tate Collins." A groupie ran by, then another, then another, all were missing various bits of their swimsuits. "Well, before I met Colorado that is," Alex amended.

"Whatever is going on, the sports sites are starting to blow up. Dallas is done for the year, just as we are. I'd heard Tate had a shitty season. Maybe his play soured over this trouble with women."

"Which is why you bi guys should stick with men, We're less prone to stirring up shit," Jacob said, pulling his man into his side to kiss him on the ear.

It was then that I excused myself and went to hide by a statue in the rose garden. Right, like men didn't do shitty things to other men. I was living proof that they did, as was Henry. My mood sank lower as I padded around the grounds letting Jean-Claude's parting words burn a bit deeper into my soul.

I want a love-air not a nan-knee, Ap-a-low!

An hour passed in wretched solitude, the music grew louder, the Raptors and rockers more boisterous. I slipped inside then slithered into the kitchen to begin the massive job of cleaning out twenty cheesy fondue pots. That was where I found Henry wedged into a corner, spooning cottage cheese out of the container into his mouth as he stared out of the window at the people milling around on the veranda and grounds.

"Your bones must be super strong," I said, his pale

blue eyes darting from the wall to me. "All the dairy you eat," I explained when he stared at me dully.

"Oh, yeah, I guess. They're healing pretty good." He put the container down then dug into a can of sliced pineapple with his fingers, lifting a ring out then taking a bite. "You throw a good party."

I padded over to the counter to deposit pots one and two. "Meh, I don't know about all that. It's been… okay." I glanced upward. He was chewing merrily, as if there weren't forty people and an emu outside. "I couldn't find you anywhere. Did you find a corner to share with some of the Penn groupies?"

Wow, that sounded snippy.

"No, I was in here for the past hour."

"Ah! I knew it. Too much touching." I nodded at my own wisdom.

"Maybe. Colorado is kind of touchy, kissy, like he feels he has to prove just how much of a rock star whore dog he can be. Besides, the party wasn't really for me anyway."

My gaze flew to him from the caked-on blue cheese in pot two. "The party most certainly *was* for you and your team."

"I thought the party was to take our minds off each other."

My thoughts flew around my head like a bird caught in a glass room. "I uhm, no, what? No. Silly, no. No, it was for… us? No, why are you saying that? There's no us."

He lifted a shoulder, taking another bite of pineapple, then another, and then another. Four bites, four quarters, all chewed and swallowed as I stood there gawking at him. There was no "us", was there? No, he was just being…

silly. Silly, handsome, sweet, lonely, sad man who needed me as much as I needed him…

I rose to my toes, sandals biting into the top of my feet, and pressed my mouth to his. Why? I did not know but in that moment, with the Moody Blues playing and the emu picking through the trash and several of the Raptors skinny dipping, kissing him felt right. He stiffened at first contact. I licked at his lower lip, picking up the sweet pineapple syrup lingering there. A fire raced through me, burning my skin, making my romper feel tight. Tighter—it was already quite form-fitting. Lust tangled with fear when his lips remained firm. Then, when I was ready to break the kiss and go jump on the emu to ride back to Harrisburg, his mouth softened. His breathing deepened, and his hands came to rest on my hips.

We tasted each other tentatively. The sweep of our tongues over the other left us ragged and twisted in each other arms, his hands on my ass, my fingers in his short hair. Then someone set off some firecrackers. Henry nipped at my lower lip then eased away. I dropped back to a flat-footed stance, my dick hard, my lips tingling, my world totally off-kilter.

"I think maybe there *is* an us," he said then eased out of the kitchen, leaving me standing there, tasting Henry and pineapple, fingers resting on my puffy lips.

SIX

Henry

TWO DAYS HAD PASSED SINCE THE KISS AND ALL I COULD focus on was how much of an idiot I'd been. Not for the kiss, but for the way I'd let emotion get the better of me.

"Morning, sunshine," Apollo called from the kitchen as I scurried past from my bedroom to the patio. I sent him a smile, but made sure to pull the glass door shut behind me. Obviously it wasn't because I wanted alone time, and more about keeping the AC in and the heat out. At least that was what I was telling myself. I couldn't even look Apollo in the eye, avoiding him, not starting conversations at dinner, citing headaches to get me into my room to the point that Apollo had threatened to call the doctor.

I think I pulled off a good act, but how could it be one hundred percent foolproof when my face got hot whenever I was near him, not least when he attempted to start conversations with me. He'd spent five minutes telling me that he'd found more emu droppings in the bushes, pausing at the end and evidently waiting for me to laugh, but I only nodded and concentrated on eating, trying to ignore the awkward silence that followed. This morning he'd created this elaborate story about how the bed in the spare room was broken and began to explain how he thought Colorado had something to do with it and how it had to be fixed for Dan visiting. I couldn't even think about my brother arriving today, so I forked up the remainder of my eggs then interrupted his speech to say I needed to go get a shower.

I think maybe there is an us?

Why had I said that? What had I been thinking? I wasn't the kind of man who made statements in case they were interpreted wrong. I'd emphasized the word *is*, implying that actually I did imagine an us, hell, I was virtually going to my knees and begging for there to be an us. Up until that moment when I'd tasted him, there had never been any solid, real idea of *us*.

Just the fantasies, just getting myself off in the shower to thoughts of him.

Oh, and watching him when he refilled the cereal bowl, and thinking he was cute-hot and kissable as he nibbled his lower lip in concentration. Or when he was changing the quilt cover on my bed and climbed inside the material to get the corners. I mean who did that? And who on this earth could make something so cute seem so damn sexy at the same time?

Of course, there was also the fact that when he cooked, made coffee, walked, talked, or indeed breathed, I found him so sexy that I was popping wood whenever he came into a room. This had to be forced proximity sexual attraction. I'd Googled it and it wasn't surprising that I couldn't get a handle on my emotions. After all, it had been a very long time since I'd actually been with a man, and that had been Aarni who'd taken great pleasure in making me feel used, and both physically and mentally intimidating me. I didn't have to be an expert to know what Aarni and I had was was all about control.

You like being safe. You need to know I'm the one in control. There had been no maybes in Aarni's subtle hints that I was a needy, helpless kid who didn't know their own mind. I'd let him say those things to me and I hadn't once argued back.

"When does Dan get here?" Apollo asked from right behind me.

I spun so fast I was off-balance and had to grip the nearest thing to stop myself from falling. Unfortunately, the nearest thing was Apollo who braced himself for my weight and helped me stay upright. He eyed me cautiously as if he was waiting for me to run, but all I did was step back and brush myself down while not meeting his gaze.

Dan was visiting with his newfound spare time, since the Philadelphia team had been beaten out of the first round of the Stanley Cup race by four games to nothing by a determined Railers team. "He texted to say he was thirty out," I said, and assumed that was enough but clearly Apollo was taking this response and running with it as if I'd started a whole new debate. I was nervous of seeing him, terrified in fact. I know he'd visited me in the hospital, all sympathy and ordering the staff to fix me, and he'd be there for me. Yes, he'd arranged with Adler for help here, but he wasn't exactly burning up the phone every day asking if I was okay. He was awkward around me, and I'm sure he feels as if he felt he didn't have a place in my life. But was that just me blocking him out?

It goes two ways, you could call him. Then my stupid psyche would convince me that Dan was better off without his stupid-ass little brother, that he'd been right to leave home to chase his dreams, and that it was my fault we weren't close.

"Do you know what you and Dan are doing?" Apollo put his hands on his hips and looked at me, and I felt like saying that Dan and I would circle each other, we'd exchange small talk, and then he'd go. "Earth to Henry? Are you going out, or do you need me to cook?"

I shrugged, then shook my head for good measure. I had things to tell Dan, warning him to keep his money away from Mom and Ed, at the same time knowing he'd never do anything as stupid as I had. Dan would be horrified, he'd think less of me, and that was what I had to face today. The thought of food, even the fantastic food that Apollo made, left me feeling sick.

"Okay, well, I'll prep some things in advance, and you can let me know, and anything we don't eat I can freeze for later." He waited for me to reply but I turned away from him.

I didn't have the capacity to talk to Apollo, not only would I make a mess of things again, but my head was too full of what I would say to Dan. He was my big brother, older than me by seven years. He hadn't gone the route of letting Mom and Ed take care of him and his finances, he'd been a real *man* and hired people through the team to take care of things for him. Then again, he'd been a first-round pick, and everything had likely been in place for him with his team. Whereas I'd worked up to the NHL level, and somehow I'd slipped through the cracks. I should have spoken to him, returned his calls, tried to get to know my big brother as an adult, but it had been him who had left me alone with her after Dad died. I didn't blame him for leaving, or at least that is what I told myself. I'd allowed myself to think it was okay for important financial decisions to be taken by Ed. So yeah, Dan and I had a lot of talking to do, and now his season was done, it was time for me to be honest about everything.

On the other hand I could pretend everything was okay as I'd done for the past few months.

"Is chicken okay?" Apollo continued, "I know one of Adler's friends has this thing about chicken, says it reminds him of squirrel, which I thought was the other way around, but then I don't want to ask why the man was eating squirrel. Come to think of it, it wasn't Dan who said that," Apollo rambled.

"We'll go out," I snapped, then was regretful as Apollo winced. "Sorry. I'm just stressed, you have every right to be pissed off at me now." God knows why I'd said that. Maybe I wanted him to demand that I grow the fuck up and stop messing him around, yell at me, and tell me that I was being a stupid ass—it was what I deserved for losing my cool. Instead he gave me a crooked smile, then patted my chest.

"It's okay," he murmured in his best soothing voice, "I get it."

Then before I could talk, he left, and guilt slammed into me that I'd snapped at him, quickly followed by confusion over what exactly he'd meant. How could he even know what was in my head right now? I mean, Jesus, he probably knew my *own* brother better than I did all because of Dan's friendship with Adler. Sulking, miserable, and with a headache forming, I stalked around the pool. Twice. Then followed a path toward the back of the garden, staying in the shade and avoiding another pile of emu poo, which I really should clear up after Dan left. Where did you put emu shit when you had it in the bag? Was it something that went in a trash can? What if I put it in there and got in trouble? Was that a civic offense? I could see the headlines now.

Hockey player fined for emu-waste transgression

Hockey player imprisoned *for emu-waste transgression*

Hockey player who can no longer play *imprisoned for emu-waste transgression*

Death row for former hockey player who'd lost all his money to his mom and had ended up with an abusive ex because he hadn't done anything about it…

My chest hurt and I pressed a hand to my breastbone as panic spiraled inside. I slumped to the ground, crossing my legs, and trying to still my breathing. What was it my therapist said, breathe, count, breathe, count, think of fluffy fucking unicorns and rainbows.

Why isn't this working?

"Hey, kid, it's okay." Dan was right by me, then he joined me on the ground, put an arm over my shoulder, and tugged me close. He'd done this in the hospital, told me things would work out in the end, but he'd sounded unconvinced then, or maybe that was just me projecting. Whatever, I hadn't believed him then and I didn't believe him now.

"You'd don't know that," I managed to force out, wriggling away from his hold and glancing up at him.

He looked confused, and I think there was hurt that I'd moved. "What can I do to help? Is there something you want to talk about? Is it your head? Do I need to call 911? Or Apollo? Or both?"

I couldn't believe my six-foot-four hard-assed hockey-playing brother was down here with me, hugging me, and speaking so soothingly. Not that he didn't have gentleness in him, but we'd always been the scrappy kind of sibling when we'd lived together, with me coming off worse. In the hospital I hadn't wanted him near me for hugs, because I hurt, and because I didn't want him to pretend to love me only because I was broken.

"No, I don't need anyone," I said, but tears clogged my throat, but fuck if I was going to sob in my brother's arms. "I don't want to talk."

"Okay, you don't have to." He moved closer and hugged me again, and this time he held firm and wouldn't let me go. "But, I'm here to listen if you need to talk, okay? Who else can you trust as much as your big brother? Huh?"

"It's been a long time since I've had a big brother," I snapped, and I instantly regretted letting my anger spill out of me, because I'd fucked up and Dan would be angry with me. I made myself as small as possible and waited for him to shout, or hit out, or worse, leave.

"I deserve that." Dan was utterly broken. "I know I fucked up, but I was always your brother. I was just lost and… fuck. When Dad died… He was the one who took us to games. Do you remember that last one? Boston were—"

"No, I don't remember any of it," I interrupted him before he could launch into fond memories of things he'd done with Dad that I would never remember. I'd only been six when he died, and I didn't have the clear memories that Dan had. "I'm sorry, carry on, I don't mean to be so…"

"Angry? You have every right to be angry with me."

I didn't want to be angry with him, after all he was the only person I had left who might have had unconditional love for me and wouldn't try to hurt me. "You left me, Dan," I said sadly, "you didn't take me with you." *Jesus, could I sound any more pathetic?* I closed my eyes tight.

"I'm sorry." His tone was so quiet, and he shuffled even closer on the hard ground. "I'm here now, and I want to start things again. When I visited you in the hospital, Henry, you looked so fragile. I remember you as this kid who held his own, and suddenly you needed me, and it scared the shit out of me to see that. I've been so used to it just being me, and I tried to make things right." He sounded frustrated. "I haven't done things the right way. Maybe I can't help you because I've fucked up in the past, but I want to try. I want to be a better brother."

He was right about not being able to help me. Who else apart from my therapist could help me? *Maybe Apollo.* I owed it to Dan to tell him about Mom, in case she had anything to do with his money. What if one day, miraculously, he decided the mom he never spoke to, along with Ed-the-asshole, should be in charge of his money? Then there was Aarni and the fact that Dan didn't know the entire story, and maybe if I told him about how pathetic I'd been then he could decide whether he wanted to be back in my life. And I wanted to talk to someone, anyone who wasn't my therapist, about Apollo and my weird lustful feelings that were about more than just about sex.

"Mom and Ed took all my money, and I can't skate because I can't see the puck, and I think I'm falling for the man who is looking after me, and is that because I'm pathetic, and you know what? I'm done." I blurted out everything in a long run.

Dan stiffened next to me. Then he picked out the first item on the list. "What?"

"Dan—"

"I brought drinks," Apollo interrupted, and startled us both, and I glanced up at him and the bright halo of sun around him as he placed a tray of ice-cold lemonade next to us. "In case you want to stay down there on the path, although we do have chairs." He gestured a few feet away to the canvas awning with the chairs underneath, then with an extra smile and a nod to Dan, he left.

"Are you okay to move, because this has been a long season, and I'm not getting any younger." Dan struggled to get up, favoring his bad knee, bruises down one calf, and I could see the brutal end-of-season matches had taken their toll on his body. All of that sacrifice and hard work and his team had been knocked out in the first round by the Railers, but at least they'd made it there—unlike my team. The Raptors were years away from a Stanley Cup run. He reached out a hand and I took it so he could help me up. He hugged me briefly, then we both sat in a chair. "Start from the beginning, Henry. Tell me everything."

"I wasn't drafted, and I… she said she'd look after the money, and when I got the contract with the Raptors, it's just a rookie contract, but it was… she took it all."

He muttered something under his breath about Mom, and I winced. "Took it how?" he asked after a small pause.

Shame burned inside me and I couldn't quite meet his thoughtful gaze. Who even let themselves get into a situation like that? Certainly not him with his house and his car and his gorgeous fiancée with a wedding planned for the summer. He had contracts worth millions, endorsement packages which meant he got thousands just from using the right gloves, or wearing the right sneakers on the weekend. He was everything I wanted to be, and it wasn't just the money, it was the aura of control that was all around him. I could've told him to leave, because he said he wanted to fix our relationship, but I could say no to that, and wouldn't have had to tell him all the secrets I carried in my heart. I sighed with feeling.

"It's my fault, I know that." Fuck, how many of my sentences started with that. My therapist said I shouldn't say that again as it framed all my words as defensive, but it was a hard habit to break. "It was easy to let her have control, and she let Ed invest it all, then lost everything and now the scheme owes money to investors. A forensic accountant is working on the details, but I don't know how much I owe, or what I'm committed to." There was a long silence, a pause while my put-together brother stared at me as if I'd gone crazy and then I saw the realization pass over his features.

"But you must've had to sign papers?"

"I did. Oscar Bledford, remember him? He would

bring them, but he promises me that he knew nothing about what Ed and mom were doing."

"Yeah, and my name is Wayne fucking Gretzky," Dan muttered. "What did the cops say?"

I ignored that question, because getting authorities involved wasn't on my to-do list right now. "Bledford is no longer my lawyer."

"Henry? Look at me." I tilted my chin and met his gaze. "What did the cops say, Henry?" He reached out and cupped my knee, and that gentle touch nearly made me cry like the kid I was inside.

"What do you want me to do?" I said miserably. "Turn my mother into the authorities?"

"She's my mom too, and Jesus, kid, if she been party of what Ed was doing, then yes."

"I'm not a kid," I defended, which was an instinctive response honed from years of people calling me *kid*. I was a grown man and I was sick of people saying that.

"No, you're not, I'm sorry. I should have stayed with you, or hell, taken you with me."

Pain made me double over and bury my face in my hands. How many nights after Dan left had I wished that he *had* taken me with him. The nights when Mom had been so intense I couldn't escape her strict rules, the nights she'd brought a new man home and declared she was in love every single time, and then the days where she'd controlled my career rigidly, from practice to money.

Then when she met Ed.

On the rare occasions I'd seen Dan, I saw his world with a ton of other options, but it was never real or available to me. First mom, then Ed, would tell me I needed to be at *this* event, or *that* practice, or to see *this* expert, and slowly but surely Dan and I had drifted apart. He was seven years older than me, we'd been at different levels in our lives for so long, and only now as I entered my first NHL year did I feel like we had something in common.

Then he went straight for the jugular, "What about your agent?"

"They had control of him as well." I was embarrassed to admit it, but mom had done so well with taking the pressure off me as I fought my way to the NHL. Then when Aarni happened, I hadn't even thought to follow any of what she was doing.

"All of it, gone?"

"Yeah. And more that I'm left to pay for."

"Shit," he said and reached for my hand, gripping it. "How do we get it back?"

The fact he used the word *we* made me feel lighter. What would it be like to have someone in my life who could help me without needing something in return? Someone who would fight my battles for me if I needed them to, but at the same time stand next to me flourishing a broad sword as we swung our way into battle. Dan and I, my brother and I, the two of us together against the world. I wanted that so badly, I'd even take just a little bit.

"I don't care about the money they took," I admitted after a pause, "I won't call the cops, and mom can have whatever she has, but I'm finished with her as long as she's with Ed."

"Henry—"

"No, that's one thing I'm certain about, the rest, the

money I owe, that's the part I don't know what to do about right now."

Dan shuffled his chair closer. "We'll fix it together," he began, "I'm sorry I left you alone. If I'd just spent less time playing and more time thinking about my little brother."

I knew he'd say something along those lines and became instantly defensive of him, but this is what I did. I excused other people's decisions even if they made my own life harder, because I didn't deserve them to…

You deserve everything.

"You had a career, what did you imagine you could do instead? Stay home for me?"

"With Dad dying, and Mom and I not seeing eye to eye, maybe, yeah." He cleared his throat. "We'll talk about Mom and what we do there. Also, I have money, more than I need, I'll transfer to clear anything owed when we have a final figure from the accountant."

"I don't—"

"No discussion, now, tell me about the rest of it. What is this about the man looking after you that you're falling for? I assume you mean the cute and sexy Apollo?"

I couldn't look at him then, because I needed to tell him about Aarni first and I didn't want talking about the sunshine and life that was Apollo to be ruined by explaining about Aarni.

"Aarni was abusive," I blurted, thinking I'd feel less of a man to admit that, but actually feeling as if a huge weight had been lifted. Dan was the first person outside of therapy that I'd really admitted it to.

Now it was Dan's turn to close his eyes briefly. "I'll kill him."

Somehow I managed a smile at the fierceness in his tone. "When the surgeon told me I might not be able to play hockey, then I could've gotten you to kill him. Hell, *I* wanted to kill him, but no, I'm to blame as well. He was the one who hurt me, and I thought I was the one who let it happen—"

"Jesus—"

"Let me finish. I know I didn't *let* it happen to me, I've had sessions with a therapist and I know deep inside that I'm not weak and that he was a manipulating partner who got off on control." Wow, that was a lot to admit to another man, even if he was my brother. Toxic masculinity was a thing and I'd been trapped because I'd allowed it to scare me from talking.

"Fucking asshole," Dan growled.

I forged ahead with what I had to say. "My eyesight issues now, being broken and twisted, that's my fault. I should *never* have gotten in the car. I should have known better. If I can't ever play again, then one day I'll be okay with that."

Dan stood so suddenly his chair flipped back, and with my hand still in his he tugged me upward into a quick hug.

"Let's go," he said and pulled me up to the house where a bemused Apollo was standing in the kitchen fiddling with bowls and spoons creating something delicious-smelling.

"Lunch?" he asked.

Dan shook his head. "Can we get it to go?"

Without blinking, Apollo pulled out containers and

packed food into a bag while I had to sit where I was told. Dan vanished down the hallway, heading God knows where. He was back ten minutes later, my hockey bags over his shoulder, grumbling about how big the house was and how the hell could anyone find anything, and adding that Adler was a rich man who cheated at hockey. Hell, we hadn't even talked about Dan's team dumping out of the Cup race, or that it was Adler's team who'd taken him down, but that was the least of my worries.

"Why do you have my gear?"

"You texted and told me you'd been back on the ice since you got out of the facility."

"Once, and it was a complete failure to—"

"Let's go," he instructed, and Apollo followed him with the food and drinks, until it was just me standing in the huge foyer, staring up at the chandelier.

"HENRY!" Dan shouted from outside.

I headed out resigned and with no hope of anything positive coming from whatever Dan was thinking. When we pulled up at the Raptors training rink, I couldn't help the groan of fear. Dan cajoled and shoved and ordered me in and finally, with Apollo watching over me, I was in skates. They were too tight, or too loose, I couldn't tell, I just knew that they felt wrong and when I hit the ice I'd fall on my ass.

I can't remember how to skate, I can't do this, I'm messed up, I can't see, and the ice is so white it hurts my eyes.

Then Dan handed me my stick with a flourish, and abruptly a sense of calm washed over me.

Apollo waited by the open gate, and I bumped his fist,

watching his beautiful smile as it turned into a wide grin. My first step on the ice was like coming home, the scent of it, the scratchy feel, the sharpness of blades, the weight of my gear, and the feel of my stick. I pushed away, glided a little, then took a step, and another, the speed picking up, Dan falling alongside me, looking odd in Raptors brown and red with Ryker's number on his back. He must have gotten it somewhere, but I didn't ask him, just thinking how funny it would be for Ryker to see that. Only it all made sense as two more skaters joined me on the ice, Ryker and his fiancé Jacob. My skating faltered a little; the last time I'd seen Ryker I'd shouted at him to leave me alone.

He did a fancy turn, iced to a stop next to me, and we fist bumped.

"Hey, eighty-three." He used my number. "Good to have you back."

"I'm not back," I protested, and glanced across at Apollo who was staring at me, still with that same smile.

"Let's do this," Dan insisted, and the four of us skated in lazy circles, from forward to backward, and knocking a puck at the net. I soon realized that I couldn't see anyone behind me, even when they were to the left. This didn't bode well, and my enthusiasm levels dipped as I missed the net on the final pass. I could give up now, in fact I skated over to Apollo for a drink, and could have easily stepped off the ice and admitted to myself I was done. Only Apollo fist bumped me again, vibrating with happiness, and then he grabbed my shirt and kissed me full on the lips in front of my brother, Ryker, and Jacob. Someone wolf-whistled and I knew I was scarlet.

"You can do this," he insisted, and then kissed me again, and this time I kissed him back. "You know what Bryan does? He's the backup goalie for the Railers who's dating that tattoo guy and—?"

"I know who Bryan is." Nice guy, another victim of Aarni's messed-up shit.

"Well, anyway, he listens to the ice."

"He listens," I repeated.

"Yeah."

Dan called me over, and I skated backward away from Apollo. *I can do that.*

It wasn't easy at first. As a hockey player I'd grown to have a sense of where people were on the ice, but that was more a visual awareness, and I was missing that. Everything was off-balance, but losing the way I used to skate was the first lesson. Ryker and I practiced passing, with Dan our third, and Jacob standing in as our temporary net minder. We skated from one end to the other, until we were exhausted, or at least until I was, and by the time we'd finished I could trust Ryker's position, and Dan's, and I connected with some of the pucks.

It wasn't perfect, but it was a start.

"Looking good, Henry!" Ryker exclaimed and side-hugged me, Jacob doing the same, before skating off to sit on the bench and watch us, then it was just me and Dan at center ice. *What now?*

He corralled a puck, then skated away from it, building up speed, heading back, and with his strongest slap shot, the stick bending, he shot the puck into the net.

"Fuck you Adler and the Railers beating us!" he

shouted, then did a little lap with a celly, fist pumping and adding a whoop.

I corralled my own puck, copied what he'd done, loving the feel of the speed, wanting more, and using every ounce of my energy, I slapped that puck right into the back of the net.

"Fuck you, eyesight!" I shouted to the rafters. Slap shot after slap shot, and with only a small break between, I was exhausted.

Fuck you, Mom! Fuck you, Aarni! Fuck everything!

And with the shooting came confidence and determination. I *could* win my life back, and it would start now. When we had showered and dressed, the five of us sat in the first row over the bench, eating bread and drinking soup, and watching the ice, all of us quiet.

Ryker broke the silence. "You looked so good out there. I know you'll be back for training camp in August."

"Easily," Dan agreed.

Then it was just up to me, and despite aching everywhere, with a headache, and blurred vision, I nodded. "Hell yes."

SEVEN

Apollo

SOMETIMES A PERSON THINKS THEY MIGHT BE FALLING FOR someone and they dilly-dally about with the tender little shoots like a gardener does his seedlings. Then there are the romances that are nothing like skinny seedings at all, they're more like the Whomping Willow where the tree picks a man up and flings him around like a ragdoll. I was right in the middle of being thoroughly whomped and it thrilled and terrified me all at once.

Henry was everything that I'd ever dreamed of in a man—tall, strong, athletic, handsome, kind, sweet, timid, bighearted, great kisser. Then again, Jean-Claude had checked all my boxes as well and look where that'd led me. So while I was dancing on air that I'd found him, I was scared shitless of being whomped by a cheating man again. Also, and this was an issue, I was being paid to be his assistant. It felt completely icky to me that I was hauling in some nice cash from Adler to flirt and kiss on the man I'd been hired to take care of.

"Why is nothing easy?" I sighed, moving through one of the four thousand bedrooms in the mansion with a feather duster in my hand. I stopped to glance outside, then, because I was prone to drifting off of late, I padded through the open doors, tipped my head back, and let the glorious sun beat down on my face. Hands on the railing, arms locked, hot desert wind tickling my cheeks, I closed my eyes and let the music from the phone in my back pocket and the sun's rays melt away my worries. "Crazy for You" hummed against my butt and a bee buzzed by my ear. Madonna's voice made me tingle, the lyrics sending shivers down my spine.

"Hey, Apollo!" Henry called. I looked down, and there he stood, shirt off, running shorts and sneakers, his skin slick with sweat, a smile on his face, back from his morning jog up in the mountains. Thank the Virgin I had a good hold of that railing, or I'd have melted to the patio like a chunk of chocolate in a locked car. "You done dusting? We have to be at the rehab center by noon."

I pulled out my phone. It was ten after nine. That made me smile like a chimp finding a banana grove. I really loved the man's quirks. With him at my side I'd never be late to anything ever again.

"Go shower, I can smell stinky man all the way up here!" I yelled down. He sniffed a pit then made a face as if he'd just smelled a skunk's ass. I howled with laughter. "Go wash. I'll be ready when you're clean."

He waved his tank top in the air then disappeared beneath me, coming through the side entrance by the gym. I lingered on the balcony for a moment or two, wondering how I'd ever managed to survive on the East coast. All the snow and ice. Ugh. I adored Arizona—the weather, the people, the food, everything. It was going to be so hard to pack up and go back to Pennsylvania in the fall. Thankfully, Henry and I had all summer.

It was already well into May, the playoffs were ramping up, and the Railers were looking to make it to the finals. I missed Adler terribly and prayed that if the Railers made it through, they'd play a west coast team so he could visit or we could fly out to see a game.

I finished the dusting then went to the kitchen to make a pitcher of *Agua de Jamaica*, a tart, sweet drink my mother prepared for the Lockhart family during the summer. I'd made it once and Henry had loved it, so now I tried to keep some on hand. I missed Mama too. I'd tried to talk her into retiring, as had Tía Sofía, but she was too stubborn and too proud to give up her role as the head of the Lockharts' domestic staff. Maybe someday her sister and I could lure her out here. She'd admitted last winter that the cold was starting to bother her hands.

While Henry showered, I got the hibiscus flowers steeping on the stove. They grew in the solarium here and the gardener, Mateo, picked them for me in exchange for a tin of *Torticas de Moron*, little Cuban sugar cookies with guava and lime filling that I baked weekly. Henry was quite fond of them as well. I'd let the flowers steep while we were gone. Then when I got home, I'd add the sugar and some cold water and chill the pitcher for dinner.

Henry met me in the airy foyer just after eleven, dressed in tan slacks, a white polo, and sneakers. Over his shoulder was a big brown duffel with a screaming raptor on the side. He slid close, pecked me on the lips, and stared down at me for the longest time.

"What? Do I have something on my face?" I wiped at my chin. He shook his head, his damp hair barely moving. "Oh I know, it's my pretty face that leaves you so besotted, isn't it?"

"Yeah, it kind of is."

"You go on." I bumped his arm with my shoulder. We strolled out to the garage then stood there side-by-side, looking at the cars parked in the cavernous space. "So, what are we feeling today?"

"The gold Alpha Romeo," he replied. So we plucked the keys from the pegboard and jumped into the luxurious sports car, me behind the wheel, him in the passenger seat. "Do the Lockharts not own regular cars like Chevy Impalas or Toyota Corollas?"

I eased her out from between a Maserati and a vintage Rolls. "No, they really don't."

Henry plugged my phone into the stereo, I put the top down, and we roared into Tucson with "Like a Virgin" blaring. The shiny mirrored sides of the Santa Catalina Arena caught my eye as we drove past. I peeked at Henry staring at the arena as if it was a long-lost lover. His mood still stayed up as we wheeled into the Draper Neurological Rehabilitation and Performance Center. This was the rehab center that Tennant Rowe had been in after his bad head injury. Henry had also rehabbed here and was now paying it back by visiting the patients, a bag filled with Raptors goodies in hand.

We entered by the side entrance, me on Henry's heels, and he glanced into the nurses' station and was hugged and kissed by many, many women. I hung back, eager to listen and watch him interact with the staff, and then later with the patients. The kids lit up when they saw him, so many Tucson residents knew him from the team. He handed out signed pucks, jerseys, T-shirts, and big plastic cups with the Raptors logo. This wasn't part of Sebastian's PR work. Seb and Alex were in the UK for the summer. Nope, this was all Henry, and it made me like him even more, if that were even possible.

"Let me take that bag out," I whispered when we'd handed out all the Raptors gear and goodies. Henry was playing a killer game of foosball with a high school football player who'd been in a car accident. "You finish the game."

He threw me a fast smile. I patted his arm, hoisted the big bag from the floor, and made my way to the nearest exit. Happy as a lark and looking forward to the ride home and all of Henry's soft smiles, I walked past the security guard seated by the big front doors.

"Hey! You with the bag. Hold up," he called. I paused, glanced back, and then froze. Mama didn't raise no foolish boys. *Anytime anyone with a badge and a gun tells you to stop, you stop, bebé*, Mama had drummed into my brown head. "Bring that bag over here and let me inspect it."

"Yes, sir," I mumbled, slowly making my way to him, the bag sliding from my shoulder to my hand. "I was just taking it to the car. I work with Henry Greenaway."

"Uh-huh, sure you do. How much you want to bet I

open this bag and find stolen goods in it?" He ripped the duffel from my hand. I eased back a step, then two, putting myself out of pistol-whipping range. As I said, Mama raised her boy to know the score. "If I find one thing in here that doesn't spell Beaner Boy on it, you're going to have a nice long talk with the cops."

"There's nothing in it. We handed out all the stuff to the patients."

He glowered at me. I pressed my lips together. "Are you mouthing back at me, Pedro?" I shook my head. He was taller than me, with thin blond hair and blue eyes. His name tag said he was Peter Marks. I said he was a swaggering, racist shitbag who wished he'd been able to pass the physical for the police academy. "You better not, *amigo*. We'll have your dirty ass back across the border before you can say taco."

"I was born in Maine," I informed him. Guess he'd had a bad day, or maybe I was just the token Latino he wanted to rough up, but before I could react properly, Mr. Rent-A-Cop had me face first into the wall, his arm around my throat.

"Did I say you could speak, you greasy little—"

He jerked hard on my neck, his forearm driving into my Adam's apple, and then there was a hearty grunt, and the security guard's hold slacked off. I coughed and gasped, spinning around while rubbing at my bruised throat, to witness Henry—my sweet, timid Henry—coming unglued on the security guard. He threw Marks into a wall then made a lunge at him, his fist drawn back.

"Stop, stop! Henry, please, stop!" I pleaded, hanging off his right arm.

He stumbled around with me dangling off his arm, his eyes burning with anger. "No one touches the man I love like that!" Henry roared. "Apologize to him *now*!"

Marks spit at me. Henry made another move to jump on the man. I somehow held him back. Nurses and visitors flocked around us. Bedlam broke out. More security guards arrived. Statements were given by me, Henry, and every POC who worked at the rehab center. Those statements about Marks and his harassment, along with the video tape footage of the encounter, were enough to ensure Peter Marks was let go. He threatened to sue Henry and me, but they were idle threats, I was sure. If he wanted to get litigious, that was fine. I knew someone who had a team of attorneys at his beck and call. I drove home, the ride a quiet one, with both of us lost in our own worlds. We pulled into the garage, cut the engine, and sat there for a whole minute.

"Henry, about that—"

"I think I want to go float."

I nodded at him. He climbed out of the car. I watched him go, my nerves shot, my stomach a jumbly mess of upset. I knew where he was going—to the pool. He loved to lie on his back in the water and stare at the sky. I usually joined him, day or night, and we would talk about things ranging from childhood traumas to which Avenger did we want to date to what kind of cat we'd be if we were in that musical. Sensing he was needing time to process, like me, I dragged my ass, and that stupid empty duffel bag, into the mansion and went to the kitchen to finish the tea and think. Chucking the bag to the floor just inside the door, I got to work. I thought better when busy. Straining flowers helped. As I stirred cup after cup of sugar into the purple-red juice, my mind kept playing over what Henry had said in the heat of the moment.

No one touches the man I love like that.

My hands started quaking. I tossed the tea into the fridge and raced upstairs. Once in my room I clambered onto the bed, touched Jesus on his bare toes, crossed myself, and asked the heavens for some divine intervention.

The afternoon was a hot one, the winds whipping down the mountains making the sheers dance madly as I sat on my bed, waiting for Jesus to get back to me, my legs in lotus position. It was taking him a long time to reply. Maybe he had more important things to tend to than the confused problems of one gay Latino man in a cute little purple romper. Probably. Like wars and tiny babies in cages along the border. Bigger stuff obviously took precedence.

The sound of a splash rolled up with the whipping winds. I slipped off the bed to peek down at Henry. He was in his green trunks, cutting through the water with strong strokes. Back and forth he went, lap after lap. Then, he stopped in the middle of the Olympic pool and went to his back, arms out, face to the sky. I changed into my yellow trunks, the ones with the pink flamingoes, and went down to join him. The smell of chlorine met me when I stepped out onto the cool, shaded tile floor of the veranda. On silent little toes I made my way to the pool, the sun hitting my back as I eased myself into the shallow end. I walked down two steps then sat, the water lapping around my chest.

Henry rolled over to his stomach then sank underwater, coming up a foot or so in front of me. Water sluiced down over his face to his chest, down his arms, and belly. We stared at each other while bumblebees worked the bright flowers and birds sang.

"I'm sorry I reacted that way," he said then reached up to run his hands over his head, squeezing water from his hair. "You looked scared."

"It wasn't fear, not really. I mean, I was scared you'd get hurt. You're still recovering, still doing physical therapy on an outpatient basis. What if that racist bastard had hit you in the head, or the eye? He could have set you back months."

He pondered that, the sun glinting off his slick skin. "So the violence didn't scare you or make you sick?"

"No, not at all. He deserved to get his ass kicked." I ran my hands over the surface of the crystal clear water.

"You want to know something?"

"Sure."

"When I defended you, it made me feel like a man. I know that's sick and twisted toxic masculinity speaking, but it really made me feel powerful to stick up for you."

I gave him a shy smile and a come-hither look that I prayed he'd pick up on. He sometimes missed visual cues if he wasn't gazing right at my face.

"This might sound sick and twisted, but I loved seeing you come to my defense. Did you mean what you said?" I peeked through my lashes. "Did you mean it when you said that I was the man you love?"

That one caught him off-guard. His beautiful eyes flared. "I don't know. It's not…"

I reached for him, hooking my finger into the band of his swim trunks.

"It's okay."

With a gentle tug he was right where I wanted him. I stood, putting myself eye to eye with him, and I wound myself around him like a vine on a strong trellis. My mouth crashed down on his, my arms went around his neck and my legs locked around his waist. His response was timid at first, the touch of the tip of his tongue to my lower lip, but then he caught fire. His hands slipped under my ass, his fingers biting into the fleshy meat as our tongues tangled.

He tasted like a new day, like a long-awaited dream about to be realized. I held on tight as he climbed out of the pool, water running off us in sheets, and carried me to the veranda, easing us down to the lounger with the soft teal cushion. I grabbed his neck, keeping his mouth locked to mine. He fit perfectly between my legs, his long body pressed into me, wet dick next to wet dick. I arched up, lapping at his mouth, as he rolled his hips, his cock sliding over mine. We both sucked in a sharp breath.

"… feel you," I gasped, nipping at his lips, my hands roaming over his head, my fingertips finding the raised scar from his wreck. I kissed him harder when I touched it, telling him that I didn't care if he had scars, I did too. His big body trembled with want. We broke apart only long enough to push our swim trunks down far enough to free our cocks. With our bodies so close, I couldn't see his prick, but I could feel it. Long, hard, resting in my hand. A shuddering moan escaped me when he began pumping his ass, rubbing his cock alongside mine.

"That's… good, so good," he panted, thrusting madly, the friction sending shockwaves to my toes. Hand on his neck, I yanked his mouth back to my lips as we ground against each other. I think I came first, hard to tell. I cried out; Henry grunted then buried his face in my neck as we rode out our orgasms. The pressure of his jaw along my throat hurt but I ignored the dull aching bruise forming. His dick kicked, spurting hot semen that mixed with mine. The tremors rolled on and on…

"So beautiful," I murmured, nudging at him so that he would lift his head. When he did I led his lips back to mine, our bellies coated with spunk, our legs tangled, one cushion wedged up and nearly over the couch's arm. "Shit that was… hot."

"Mm hmm, you're hot, beautiful." He nipped at my lower lip then slowly peeled himself off me. We were a damn mess, cum smeared all over us, but we were smiling. "Come on, I'll wash you off."

I got to my feet, stepped out of my shorts, and clambered right back over him like a horny monkey scaling a sexy palm tree. With a snort he wiggled around, holding me close, until his trunks slithered down his legs. He left them on the veranda. With me plastered to him, he jogged down to the pool, dick bouncing and slapping me on the ass—yum—and walked us out into the pool one step at a time, his mouth moving over mine as the water got higher and higher. When the water was under my chin, he stopped, his feet still on the cement bottom.

"You're really special to me," he whispered as water lapped around us.

"You're really special to me too."

"You make me feel safe and cared for."

"I'm glad. Kiss me again, just so I can make damn sure of how special the feelings are."

He did. Yep, I was. Damn sure and scared absolutely out of my mind.

EIGHT

Henry

LORRAINE HANDED ME A BLINDFOLD.

"What is this for?" I didn't even want to think why she was handing me a blindfold in the middle of an exercise room.

"Sensory deprivation," she announced, but that didn't make sense because surely, with my eye as messed up as it was, I was already deprived of full eyesight.

"I'm confused."

"Actually you look horrified," she chuckled. "Think *Star Wars* hero more than *Fifty Shades* kink," she explained.

"Huh?" Nope, none of that cleared this up.

I wasn't sure what worried me more, that she'd mentioned kink, or that I had absolutely no freaking idea of what she was talking about. Moreover, I heard Apollo snigger in the corner of the room where he was in the lotus position on a pile of yoga mats. Just the sound of his laughter made me think all kinds of X-rated things I could do with a blindfold, and I had to employ all my will to stop getting hard in my loose jogging pants.

"Okay, this is what we're doing, I'm going to use this." She held up the ball—a soft foam sphere in luminous green. Then she handed me a piece of plastic in the shape of a tiny hockey stick. It looked as if the whole thing might have been a hockey set designed for a toddler, and nope, I still wasn't getting it. "I'm going to stand here and toss the ball at you and you are going to bat it away. Like this." She tossed the ball at me and caught me by surprise. It bopped my nose and rolled to the floor.

That sounded easy enough, and when she threw the next ball I tracked with my good eye to where she was standing, easily batted it away, and felt like a proud kid in their first nativity. I was rocking this bat and ball thing.

"Now put the mask on," she said, and held the ball close to her chest.

"Then I can't see."

"That is the point. I'm taking away all of your eyesight and you are going to listen to me, to the ball, feel the weight of the soft stick in your hands, and I want you to talk to me and tell me what you're feeling."

I glanced over at Apollo, not sure I wanted him to witness me in a blindfold waving blindly at a foam ball. Maybe it was my expression, maybe it was his own compassion, but he uncurled himself, and with a wave he opened the door. "I need coffee," he lied, and closed the door behind him. Now I was alone with Lorraine, the mask, and the kids' hockey set, and I felt apprehensive. More than that, I was scared. My worst nightmare was losing my sight, and at first I'd been unaccountably relieved that it was only one eye that had been affected, until of course, the reality of that had hit me like a one hundred mile an hour puck.

"Talk to me," Lorraine said, and I realized she was staring at me, waiting for me to put on that damn mask.

"I don't like not being able to see."

She stepped close to me, and took the mask from me. "I understand that, and it won't be for long. Five minutes, that's all, and you can stop any time."

What was I doing? I was being such a weak person, not even wanting to put a mask on.

You can't even have sex without me telling you what to do. My chest tightened as Aarni's words smacked into me but I answered the words in my head, *I didn't seem to have a problem at the pool with Apollo, did I?* Then the self-doubt slipped in and suddenly I was back there, recalling the moment that had led to us going to the chairs, and was that me? Had I done that? Or had he told me to pick him up?

"Henry? Henry! Look at me." I blinked at Lorraine, and she held out the mask. "You can stop if you want to." Sudden steel straightened my spine. Dan would be proud of me for working so hard.

Apollo will be so pleased.

Carefully, I passed her the stick and slid the mask over my head, taking one last look at her kind eyes before it all went black. My skin prickled with fear, and my breathing hitched and then settled as Lorraine calmed me.

"Just breathe, in, out, in, out…"

I gripped the stick, listened to her words, knew where she was standing.

"I'm ready," I murmured.

"I'm here, just in front of you, I'm going to toss the ball on the count of three, try to contact it, listen to my voice, and my movements. In three. Two. One. Go."

The ball bounced off my chest, a lighter than air touch that nevertheless made me jump, even as I swung the stick.

"Shit." I couldn't help my disappointment.

"Tell me how you feel?"

"Pissed at myself for missing it."

"You swung on zero, maybe you should swing on the G of go? You want to try that? Let's try. Three. Two. One. Go."

I did what she said but again the ball hit me, and yet again I cursed as frustration built inside me. *Fucking useless.* "I can't do this."

"How about on the one?" She ignored my lack of positivity. "Listen to my words, and go on the one. Three, two, one, go."

I swung on the one, felt the contact, the soft weight of the ball bonding with the plastic for a second, and the flex of the stick as it touched.

"Yes!" I said, and let out a little whoop of joy.

"Again, three, two, one, go."

I connected again and again, and then missed some, getting too cocky, swinging on the two, swinging on the G, trying all kinds of timings, but it was always on the one that I connected and I wondered what this was teaching me.

"Now I want you to listen to my voice," she said, and the words moved around the room as she was walking,

"I'm in another place in the room, can you tell where I am?"

That was easy. She was behind me, and I turned to face her. Batting the ball each time she threw it.

"Now, I'm not going to count, I'm just going to throw. Ready?"

I was confused, how would I know when to swing? The ball hit me square on the chest, and I cursed. "I can't tell when you're throwing it, how am I going to know when to try and hit it?"

"Listen to the noise, the brush of the cotton on my arm, the air displacement, my breathing. Let's try again."

I listened as hard as I could. The next four balls bounced harmlessly off of me, but I refused to give up. I could sense the movement, the slide of cotton, the way her breathing would subtly change, and in my head I created my own three, two, one, go. I hit ball five so hard that it indicated I'd gone way too fast with the swing. Ball six was better. Ball seven was the perfect meeting of plastic and foam.

"Okay, you can take off the mask," she said.

"But I was doing really well."

"Which is why we're ending this now, on a high. We'll do some more next session, but I want you to close your eyes at various times and concentrate on the world around you, listen to the subtle noises."

Listen to the ice. Isn't that what Apollo said I should do? I could do that if it meant getting back on my skates.

Apollo was quiet as we went back to the car, but I couldn't help talking because I was high on life. "… and then I hit it so hard that I swear even that tiny foam ball would have left a hole in the wall. It's all about sensory awareness, and I guess if I have the trust in my line to be in the right place at the right time, I don't need to see them to know they are there. A blind pass, back through my legs, trusting that my guys have my back. This could really work, and maybe I don't have to worry so much about the cloudiness? I mean, it's early days, and it was just a stupid ass foam ball and a kid's plastic hockey stick, but you never know, right? I could move up to pucks."

I climbed into the car and waited until Apollo had his belt on, ready to tell him more about how I was feeling and what I was doing, and how everything in my universe was sunshine and fucking rainbows, and then I read his expression.

"What? What happened? Are you okay? Is Dan okay? Talk to me."

Instead of talking he passed over the cellphone he'd been clutching, unlocking the screen and allowing me to read a headline from a hockey blog that specialized in stories featuring the more gossipy side of hockey.

"On the pressure of fame," I read out loud, then glanced at Apollo. "What is this?"

"It was just posted," Apollo murmured, and gestured for me to read on.

So I did, "Losing his spot on the Raptors was one thing that Aarni Lankinen… what the fuck?" I glanced at Apollo. "Why are you making me read this?" He appeared to be heartbroken, his dark eyes shining with tears. Why was Apollo so upset? What could possibly be so bad that he looked as if his world had been turned upside down? I read on, out loud for the most part. "When I interviewed the burly defender, he made it clear he had regrets after that day. In fact he told us in his own words… it all ended the day I crashed a car, causing my passenger to be hurt, and it is something I regret, but that I don't have words for. I was in love with Henry, and for all his faults I honestly believed he was in love with me too. When he asked me to drive him home—" I stopped, re-read that part, and then carried on, this time silently.

I don't know why Henry wanted to go home so early that day, but he said he needed to take his meds. I don't know what his meds were for, although he was coming down from a puck to the knee, so maybe opioids, but don't quote me on that…

I closed the article without reading any further, then sat in absolute silence. I'd never taken anything stronger than Tylenol in my entire damn life until the hospital had to put my broken body back together. Opioids? Fuck. What if the team saw this? Worse, what if they believed what Aarni was saying in what was subtitled *an intimate article from the mind of a man under pressure.* Pressure? Aarni didn't know anything about pressure. All he knew was control, and he was still doing it now from beyond the limits of any relationship we once had.

"Henry?" Apollo asked cautiously, but I was gentle when I handed the phone back.

"I need to go home."

"What can I do? Should we call someone?"

"I want to go home."

"Henry, please, we should call someone. The team? You can't just take this lying down."

You have no backbone on the ice or off, you're a

coward. Aarni was in my head again, like a virus infecting every part of me, and what was the actual point of me saying anything to the team? This was out there, and it didn't matter that most people knew Aarni had been drunk, after all it was public record, but there would be those people out there… staring at me, thinking it was my fault.

"I'm not taking it lying down," I snapped the words so forcefully that Apollo shrank back away from me, and guilt consumed me. "I'm no better than him!" I blurted and he reached for me. I was a mess of contradictions, and I was no good to Apollo like this. I fought with the door handle and tumbled out of the car, striding away from anything that could be good in my life. Heading where, I don't know, but at least I could breathe. Who did Apollo want me to call? Who the hell could stop Aarni from saying anything he wanted and a whole bunch of people believing what he said?

Apollo didn't come near me but I could hear the car following me at a distance, but at the single moment when I thought I would give in and get back in, I called for a cab instead. Apollo watched me from where he parked, then followed me home. It was stupid, I know that, it was childish and hateful, and I was hurting one of the only people who listened to me and made me feel as if I could be special. I went inside the huge house, wondering which room to hide in, but Apollo was right there, and he was waving a phone in front of my face.

"It's for you," he said, and made as if he was going to drop it, so I took it from him.

At first it didn't make sense who was on the screen in this FaceTime, because I was looking through a cloud of self-hatred and anger, and then it made complete sense, and the ice around my heart cracked a little. Someone else who had been on the receiving end of Aarni's manipulation, the other person who could really know what I was feeling.

"Bryan," I murmured.

He had marks on his face where his goalie mask had pressed into the skin, and he was sweating as if Apollo had called him out of practice, and the Railers blue was a soothing comforting thing.

"Tell him," a voice came from behind Bryan, and I recognized Adler. "Make it right."

"Leave us alone, Ads," Bryan said, then he was walking, and finally he was in a quiet space leaning against a door. "Hi, Henry, how are you doing?"

"I don't know," I said, with so much misery in my voice that Bryan winced.

"Sit down, Henry. Is Apollo there with you now?"

I glanced to my left where Apollo stood looking as if he were expecting me to scream at him for what he'd done. How did he know what to do here? How had he known to call Bryan? My heart filled with hope, and I extended a hand to Apollo who took it and held it firmly. Then we sat on the sofa, close together, and Bryan began to talk.

NINE

Apollo

SITTING BESIDE HENRY, HIS BIG WARM HAND CLASPING mine, I listened and cried soft, quiet tears. Of course I could see Bryan, and listen to what he said, but I didn't say a word. It wasn't my business. The two men barely knew each other yet they shared a common bond. They'd both been abused by the same man. Sniffling madly as the whispered conversation went on, I worked on slipping my hand free of the tight grip Henry had on it.

I pointed to my running nose then at the box of tissues across the room. He nodded. Rising from the sofa, I slid my fingertips over his, then his hand dropped to the couch. The tissue run was a necessity. Sneaking into the kitchen to pour us both tall glasses of *Agua de Jamaica* then puttering around with a plate of *Torticas de Moron* wasn't a necessity at all. It was an excuse to splash water on my face, gather myself, and give Henry and Bryan privacy. When I returned with our drinks and Henry's new favorite cookies in the world—his words not mine—he was sitting with the phone on his thigh, his gaze locked on the stone fireplace.

"It took you twenty-five minutes to make drinks," he pointed out, his sight moving to me as I placed the tray on the coffee table.

"I'm sorry. I felt like a creeper listening to that conversation." He sighed then held out his hand. I took it, sitting with a leg tucked under me. "Did it help? Talking to him? I hope I didn't overstep my bounds as your…" I bumbled around, mentally looking for the right word. I'd signed on as a companion but we'd taken things way past a simple cook/light housekeeping/caretaker relationship. We'd had that moment on the veranda. That had made everything different in so many ways. "I'm not sure what we are anymore."

"No, me either. I know my days are sunnier with you in them."

Yes, mine were too. *"Amigos Soleados."* He stared at me in confusion. "Sunny friends."

He nodded. I wiggled my fingers free long enough to pour our drinks and offer him some cookies. Then I curled into his side, nibbled on a cookie, and sipped the sweet hibiscus tea as his fingers toyed with mine. Friends. I didn't want to be friends with him, not really. I wanted more with him despite knowing I shouldn't.

"Thanks, for calling Bryan. That really helped."

"Anytime. All I want is to see you happy and healthy," I said around a bite of cookie.

"That's the same way I feel about you, Apollo."

He pressed a kiss to my ear as I pushed play on *Evita*, a

movie Henry had never seen before. It was a simple gesture, nothing grand or erotic, but it was steeped with tenderness and a warm familiarity that set off a wild chain reaction of emotion deep within me. I sucked in a breath, held it, and let it out, but was still certain that with a simple peck to my ear I'd tumbled madly in love. I shoved the cookie in my hand into my mouth, chewed, then began to have a silent panic attack. I gobbled down cookie after cookie and then more cookies to try to smother the terror falling in love had stirred up. Just about the time that Antonio Banderas was singing "High, Flying Adored" I reached for the last cookie on the platter.

Henry playfully made a grab for it as I lifted it to my mouth. The tiny treat fell from my fingers to my lap and Henry grabbed at the cookie. His hand moved over my cock as we battled for the sweet between my legs. It was as if the sky opened up and a lightning bolt of want, lust, fear, and love danced downward to the earth, hitting the two of us at the same time. I couldn't say how Henry felt, but I knew that I'd forever be singed. His sky-blue eyes met mine, the cookie forgotten, as his fingers slid over my thickening prick.

"Fuck that cookie," I grunted, pushing my sugar-sticky fingers into his hair.

He palmed my cock as I yanked his mouth to mine. The movie, the cookie, the world fell away when his tongue slid over mine. The kisses we shared were wet, hot, deep explorations mingled with tender pecks and soft, breathy exhalations. Hands tugged and pulled at clothing, his big body pressing me down into the sofa as I wiggled out of my underwear, desperate to feel his warm skin next to mine.

"God, you're so soft," he groaned, mouthing his way along my shoulder then down to my chest. He flicked a nipple and I cried out; our cocks pinned between us, leaving slick trails over our bellies. "So smooth. No hair anywhere…"

"Do you like me soft and smooth?"

"Yeah, oh yeah. I like you soft."

"And you're so hard," I countered, slipping my hand between us. I found his cock with ease, took it in hand, and stroked him madly. "Come for me, come on me, come in me."

"God, Apollo I… shit." He ground into my grip then pulled free, easing himself down over me, his mouth skimming over my belly and sides then back to my mouth. It was a frenzied tangle of arms and legs, fingers grasping, mouths seeking. The man needed to get into me now, right now, before I came unglued and blew apart without feeling him deep within me.

"Lube, something… spit, butter, cookie filling, I don't care! Just get inside me," I begged, writhing under him, our dicks ramming into each other's, each pass making my balls tighten and tingle. "I'm so close, please. Ah, Henry, I have to have you in me. Please, *te amo*. I love you, Henry, fuck me, make me yours."

"Okay, yes, okay, just… one second." He stole a sloppy kiss then moved to the side, pawing on the floor for his shorts. "I think… I'm not sure how old it is, I mean… ouch, your knee is in my nut sac."

"Sorry, oh hell, sorry, baby. Do you have lube in your wallet?"

"Yeah and a condom, we need a condom."

I moaned at the mention of a barrier between us. He found what he was looking for—a lone condom and a packet of lube. I whispered my thanks to the heavens then helped him smear slick all over his latex-covered cock.

"Oh okay stop, please, stop," he huffed. "I'm too close," he coughed out. I released his cock then slid my fingers down between my legs to work some lube into me. Henry made this gruff sound that sent shivers down my spine. I worked those two fingers in and out of my hole as he kneeled between my thighs watching. "Me, let me in now."

"Fuck yes!" I pulled my fingers free, planted my heels on the cushions, and levered my ass up off the couch. The round head of his cock entered me. I gasped, the stretch and burn intense as it had been so long. "Do not stop. Fill me up with your cock. Yes, mmm, shit, yes. Ah!"

He pushed deeper, past that ring, and then was sliding into me, inch by inch, his hands wrapped around my ankles, he slowly claimed me until he was seated fully. We both were panting, sweaty, on the cusp of tumbling into an abyss. Or perhaps that was just me. I loved him, I knew it, and I wanted him forever. But this was not a forever arrangement, it was a summer job, a romance that would only survive until the leaves began to color. Then he'd be back on the ice for training camp and his need for me would be gone. I squeezed my eyes shut to hide the tears.

"Am I hurting you?" he asked, dropping over me, his hands on either side of my head, my knees now resting on my chest. "Please tell me if I am."

"No, no, never. Love me now, fast, hard, make me yours, Henry."

"God, Apollo." He leaned down, licked into my mouth, and started thrusting. There was no time for slow, no need for a build-up. We were both tottering on the precipice before he'd pushed that long, hard dick into me. "God, I never…"

"No, baby, me… either." My fingers bit into his biceps. The couch grated over the flooring, pillows tumbling off, the lamp on the end table wobbling then falling. He pumped hard, stealing my breath as he did my heart and soul. Who came first was difficult to say, I grabbed my dick as the first pulse of cum flew from me. Henry groaned low and long, driving into me one final time, his cock kicking deep inside me. Fingers coated, I jerked on my cock, milking it as my ass tightened around my lover, squeezing his dick. He buckled after the last shudders subsided, his mouth crashing down over mine. My tongue tangled with his.

"Holy shit," he whispered, kissing my lips then my nose then my chin before easing himself out and sliding an arm around my back. With a grunt, he hoisted me up then fell back to the couch, my sticky belly and chest mashed to his. I stole a hundred kisses while muttering silly little Spanish things to him as the cool air from the mountains wafted over us, chilling us both. "Oh man, that was the best ever. You're so… I like you so much."

Lying there on him, the smell of sex curled around us like a sensual blanket, I blinked back tears as Madonna belted out "Don't Cry for Me Argentina" and Antonio watched from the crowd. That would have to be me someday, a face in the crowd, as Henry's recovery and future fame carried him and I apart.

A WEEK LATER, WHEN HENRY WAS IN THERAPY PRETENDING to be a budding Jedi, I went to visit Tía Sofía at work. The offices for Queenly Color Cosmetics were in the heart of downtown Tucson right by the Bank of America Plaza. She was expecting me as I'd called this morning while Henry had been showering, and begged her to see me *today* before I ate any more cookies. My rompers and skinny jeans were getting tight. To say that I was freaking out over my leap off the ledge of sanity into the deep, dark pools of love was an understatement. I was in a full-fledged romantic meltdown.

Running on sugar and fear, I parked in a reserved spot in the QCC parking area, giving zero fucks about who the vice-president was. I was the president's nephew and I was spiraling here!

Recalling my past trips here, I rode up to the top of the skyscraper, bolted out of the elevator, and raced as fast as my flip-flops would allow to the executive offices. Tía Sofía was in her corner office, sipping hot tea as the city of Tucson hustled and bustled below. Her hair was piled up on her head and she was in a bright yellow sundress that had lime slices all over it. Her heels were green as the limes on her dress.

"Your nephew is here," Ramona shouted as I flipped and flopped into the spacious suite.

My aunt looked at me over the top of her computer monitor. "The boy does love his dramatic entrances," Tía Sofía said then laughed softly. "Ramona, go get the child a cup of green tea, decaf." Ramona, who was older than the wooden Jesus on my bedroom wall, went shuffling off to make tea. "She'll be back in about twenty minutes or so, maybe with tea, maybe without."

"Why do you keep her on? She's got to be a hundred and twenty," I snapped, pacing around the room, my flip-flops flopping and my silver bangles bangling.

"Because she was one of the first trans people I met when I moved out here. Without her and the other LGBT elders in this city I'd still be a lost, little Hispanic boy who could only dream of being the girl he knew he was supposed to be. Is that a good enough reason?"

I paused by the huge windows and let my brow drop to the thick glass. "Yes, of course, I'm sorry for being a bitch about Ramona. I think I'm in love."

"With a man?" I lifted my head to toss her a "Really?" look then let my forehead drop back to the glass. "Well I had to ask. The way you're flailing around this morning I thought you'd fallen in love with that tiger from the Disney movie that scared you when you were a little boy."

"No, Aunty, I am *not* in love with Shere Khan. And for the record he wanted to eat Mowgli, so yeah, I was scared of him. Big cats that have a fondness for brown boys are scary."

She giggled into her tea. "Why don't you sit down over at the sample table?" I sighed dramatically but did as she asked. She placed her tea on her desk, rose in a gracious manner, and walked over to the long white table by the wall. "Let's try out some of these new foundations on you. You're a lighter shade than I am and I'd like to have a few choices when they go to marketing." I held out my arm and she sat beside me, crossing one long leg over the other as she unscrewed a gold lid from a smoky white round bottle. "They're not named yet, of course, but this one is X-18, which might match your skin tone." She dabbed a finger into the jar and began rubbing the cover-up onto the inside of my left forearm. "Hmm, no, it's too light."

"Tía Sofía, I'm happy to help with makeup, you know that, but I need to tell you about my fickle heart."

"You pickled your heart? Oh, that's not wise, Apollo." I caught the glimmer of mischief in her brown eyes. "Oh, baby, don't scowl so. It'll give you premature wrinkles."

"Tía, I think I fell in love with Henry. No, that's too dark," I said when she applied another color to my arm. She nodded in agreement. "I vowed after the last time with that shitass dickhead whose name shall never cross my lips—"

"You could use some lip color too, are you not using the gloss I sent you?"

"Tía Sofía, *please*! I'm telling you that your favorite nephew—"

"My *only* nephew," she corrected then dabbed a dollop of foundation above the other two round patches and rubbed.

I huffed. "Which makes me your favorite. I broke my own promise to myself, and to Jesus, and let myself fall in love with Henry knowing this was a summer job."

"Hmm, this soft acorn is closer but not quite. And what's wrong with loving Henry? He's a delightful young man who's obviously smitten with you."

"*What's wrong?*"

"There's no need to shout, I'm sitting right here."

"Sorry, yes, I know you are. Try that one there." I

pointed to a bottle toward the back of the table. "No, yes, that one. That might be close."

"Good choice. So, the end of the world is about to fall down on us because you have feelings for Henry. Shall I book us passage on a cruise ship so that when the skies fall and the earth cracks open, we'll be out on the ocean and avoid the Armageddon that Jesus will surely send us because one little gay boy fell in love with another little gay boy?"

"I'm not sure why you're being such a sarcastic cow right now."

"Because, Apollo, you're overreacting. Yes, Jean-Claude was a rotten pig bastard, but Henry isn't Jean-Claude, he's Henry. That boy wouldn't harm a fly."

"You didn't see him go after that security guard," I mumbled, poking at the lip gloss tubes lying among the concealer and false eyelashes.

"He did that to save you, *mijo*."

"Well, yeah okay, he did. God that was amazing. I've never had a man go berserk like that over me, but still I'm leaving in September. And then I'll be back in the shadows and cold with another broken heart! Ah! Why do I do this to myself?"

She tapped my nose with the glop of concealer that I'd pointed out. "Hysterical does not look good on a man, Apollo. Why are you so sure you'll be leaving? Don't you love it here?"

"Yes, but Henry's need for me will be over when he's back to one hundred percent. I can't just stay here in Tucson!"

"Why not? Henry cares about you, you love the city

and the weather, and your favorite aunt is here." I started to argue that Henry didn't love me. He'd never once said so, aside from in a moment of berserker rage and that didn't count. We'd made love and he'd only said he liked me. Liked. Not loved. "… crazy about you. The others were just using you because you're so pretty and so eager to coddle them. So many men are looking for lovers to replace their mothers and so they leap on any man or woman with a nurturing heart. They didn't love you, not really, they loved the mothering that you gave them. He cares for you."

"Henry needs me too, though," I pointed out, smoothing the dot of concealer across the bridge of my nose.

"Yes, but not as a mother substitute. He needs you for other reasons like companionship, laughter, caring, and passion, and you need him for those same reasons. Apollo, honey, stop letting fear rule your life. One or two bad relationships don't mean you should never care for another man ever again. It just means that you have to guide your heart to choose more wisely."

I sat there for a moment or two, thinking as she patted some powder over the concealer she'd just applied to my arm.

"Do you think my heart has chosen wisely? I'm so scared of being hurt again," I asked, my throat thick and my eyes dewy.

"I think your heart has chosen *very* wisely."

I threw myself at her, hugging her around the neck. She rubbed my back with her free hand. The door opened and Ramona toddled in with a paper napkin and a can of tomato juice. My aunt and I shared a sigh and a can of tomato juice. When I left an hour later, I had a new look and a new attitude about my feelings for Henry. Mostly new. Somewhat new. Sort of new, but also moderately shaky.

When Henry saw me sitting on a bench outside his PT offices, his blue eyes went round as manhole covers.

"Wow, you… wow. Makeup."

I batted my super long and thick lashes. "I went to see Tía Sofía at work. We might have dabbled with the products. Do you like me with makeup on? Some men do and some don't."

"No, I like it. Your lips are so pink and sparkly." He sat beside me, his aura calm and strong, as it tended to be now after his therapy sessions.

"Do you want to kiss them?" I teased, puckering up like a fashion model.

"Yeah, I do." He leaned in and put his lips to mine. They slid right off. We both laughed at that. "Maybe you need a little less next time."

"Maybe so," I sniggered, using my thumb to wipe the hot pink gloss from his lips. "You look happy, Henry."

"I am. That's kind of due to you. You make me so happy, and safe."

I felt a blush creeping up my neck and was about to tell him that I thought—no, I was pretty sure—that I was in love with him when a group of guys ran up to us. Fans obviously as they were all wearing Raptors T-shirts.

"Next season is going to rock!" one of the young men hooted, clapping Henry on the shoulder. The others began talking at once, all excitedly and falling over the others, as

Henry and I sat there looking confused about the energy. "I was kind of silently praying they'd get him and they did!"

"Dude, like honestly, he tucked his tail and left Dallas and his wacko ex-fiancée behind. I mean, I'm totally down with him being a Raptor because he's going to plug up that first line hole in the middle, but shit, what kind of dude runs out on his team because some chick slaps down another chick in public?"

"Whoa, dude, no way does Collins get that first line spot from Madsen!"

"Oh fuck you, of course he will!"

"Wait, slow down guys," Henry said, standing to speak. "Are you saying that the Raptors *signed* Tate Collins from Dallas? The last I heard they were mid-summer rumors."

Six cellphones were jammed into Henry's face. Of course as he read, I was doing the same thing. In a sweeping move the Raptors management had somehow lured superstar Tate Collins to Tucson. It had cost them $81.2 million dollars to secure the upcoming free agent for seven years. I had to read that salary hit several times to make sure my new eyeliner hadn't smudged into my eyes and caused me to see a fake number. Nope. It was right there on several sites—$81.2 million for seven years. Holy shit. I guess the Westman-Reids weren't monkeying around with this rebuild. Of course they'd given up some top draft picks, but Collins was only twenty-five and had a lot of years of high production left in him.

"Damn," Henry whispered as he sat down after the rabid fan boys had run off to celebrate the arrival of Tate in Tucson, come September. "Did the owners have to sell body parts to afford that massive contract? And what about us smaller guys? Is there any money left after a cap hit like that?"

"I'm sure they know what they're doing. Don't worry over things you can't control."

"Right, yeah, you're right, it's just… wow, Tate Collins. I'm not sure I'll ever be able to heal enough to play beside someone like that."

I wiggled closer, took his chin in my hand, and stared into his worried gaze. "You are an amazing man and can do anything that you put your mind to. Trust me on this, those big names like Collins and Madsen-Rowe all put their pants on the same way you do."

Then I kissed him, right on the mouth in the open where the world could see it. This time our lips stayed together and I melted into the strong arms that tightened around me.

"I love how you always say the right things," he murmured over my puffy lips when the kiss broke. "You're my personal sun that I can hold in my arms."

"Begone shadows," I whispered then pulled him closer for another taste.

TEN

Henry

THE GROUP CHAT WENT WILD, AND BY THE TIME I'D caught up with everything that'd been said and done in there about the whole Tate thing, I was dealing with a headache and the nagging concern that the Raptors might tear itself apart as a team. On one side of the debate was Ryker, Jens, and Alex saying how they were all super-stoked, and that Tate was another piece in the puzzle that was the team rebuild. I could tell they'd all had rookie media training, because even in a group chat they were diplomatic. But some of what happened was funny and I wanted to tell Apollo everything, so I moved onto the other side of the argument.

"And then Colorado said that he loved shoving Tate on the ice just for shits and giggles and that Tate had lost his cool last time they played against each other, and that had wound Colorado up badly. So, Ryker was all blah blah PC, and maybe Colorado shouldn't have wound the man up in the first place, and then it was so funny because Vlad went supernova on the whole conversation."

"Vlad is a good captain," Apollo interjected.

"Yeah, but seriously, I've never seen Vlad come down so hard on the team as he did in that chat, he was all *support this* and *understand that*, and even Colorado backed down in the end. Listen to what Jens said—"

Apollo swiped the phone off me and placed it flat on the counter, turning it off and placing his hand over it. "No more reading," he announced, and I was mesmerized by the tiniest fleck of glitter on the outside corner of his eyes. He'd asked me what I thought about a guy wearing makeup, and to be honest I'd not thought about it before, but Apollo with the gloss and the eyes and the glitter, I'd been so turned on it was ridiculous. Every sweep of color had made his features pop and he was gorgeous.

"I was just looking at the chat."

"It's not good for you."

"I'm fine," I lied.

"I can see you screwing up your eyes, and the specialist warned you that you shouldn't stare at a screen for more than ten minutes at a time. Not to mention you get upset when you see a new comment on that Aarni article."

Oh yeah, that. It was a thorn in my side, and I was toying with doing my own article. Adler had suggested we sue Aarni for defamation or whatever, but I didn't want to think about it more than I already did. I shouldn't even have checked the post, but for every ten comments talking about me and how I was the victim, there was one who remembered Aarni as 'a helluva player' and that 'he'd been wronged'.

"Okay, I won't read anymore," I promised, although I

picked up my phone and at his frown placed it very deliberately into my pocket. Then, I hovered around the kitchen for a short time as Apollo did something fancy with a green pepper and ginger. But it was obvious he wasn't interested in hearing my summary of the team opinions on Tate Collins joining us for training camp, or the impact on the cap limit. Who could blame him? Unless a person played hockey they wouldn't understand how a skater at the same skill level as Tennant Madsen-Rowe, if not better, would impact us. With Ryker and his line, and now Tate building his own line, the Raptors could have a one-two punch that would give both centers the chance to shine. It was exciting, but at the same time it was nerve-wracking.

Because after the initial excitement, all I could think was, where did this leave me? And I wasn't even thinking about my injury, this was all about the fact that I am a solid winger who'd already lost my chance at a place on Ryker's wing now he was part of the famous Jens-Alex-Ryker JAR line. That was where I had always hoped to be, playing with Ryker and Alex.

And I fucked it all up by getting in the car with Aarni.

If my eye healed or there was a miraculous intervention, or even if I worked so hard that I found my rhythm with the team as Coach wanted, I wasn't going to be fast enough to be at Tate's side. I'd be third line, possibly fourth, and that was a vulnerability in my future that left me feeling hollow.

At least talking out loud about what the other guys on the team thought, meant I could vocalize my own fears without looking like a self-pitying idiot. Half the team weren't happy with the idea of Tate in the team, the other half were diplomatic, and Vlad was thunderously shutting us all down. With Tate on our team we had a chance to make it off the bottom of the league, and underneath all the bitching and worries, at the end of the day it was all about the team doing well.

I wandered around the house, through the bedroom, and the spare rooms, and the atrium, and the balcony, and down into the largest room that I'd dubbed the ballroom. It was at least fifty feet long and just as wide—a huge space with high ceilings and a partition wall that could be moved to split the room in two. It had become somewhat of an exercise room for me; an absolutely empty space where I worked drills. The kind that had me running from one end of the other and stopping on a dime before heading back the same way. At each end there were large open windows, the front overlooking an ornate fountain and the edge of the drive as it curved around, the back with a gorgeous view of Tucson and beyond.

Energy sparked inside me and I bounced on my toes, doing a couple of cartwheels and walking a short way on my hands. I wasn't flexible like Apollo—he was all lithe movement and bendiness. Whereas I had a typical skater's ass, thick heavy muscles, and was bottom heavy. I toppled easily, but tried again, until I managed at least six hand steps, then I flipped upright and fought the head rush. Part of my thought process was that somehow this could shake parts of me loose, like the curtain that hung over my eye, or the muscles that ached in my shoulders, even if my therapist told me I was *an idiot who doesn't understand the dynamics of an eye injury.*

"Hey, Henry," Dan said from the door. He'd been a visitor on more than one occasion since my breakdown in the garden, only this time he wasn't alone. An older man—tall, skinny, with huge round glasses—stood next to him, looking all kinds of official in a smart suit and tie.

"I was just stretching out," I explained, hoping that made sense.

"Cool, look, this is Miles Butler, can the three of us go somewhere and talk?"

I crossed to Miles and shook his hand, he appeared to be about sixty, with a shock of white hair, and the air of someone who was confidently in charge of life.

"Henry Greenaway," I said as we shook and I glanced at Dan who wouldn't quite meet my gaze. "What is this about?" I asked my reticent brother, who finally looked me in the eye and tilted his chin.

"Forms to sign, that kind of thing," he said, daring me to ask him more questions. We might have drifted away from being brothers in the truest sense but I could see the determination in Dan's eyes, so with the headache still there, I decided to go with the flow. I took them through the solarium tacked on the back of the house, with the heat of the day countered by the shade of short-ass palm trees inside, and the iciness of underfloor cooling, and we ended up in the room that I had commandeered as my space to store all my hockey stuff. I felt at ease in this room, as if I belonged in there.

Miles cleared his throat and I paid attention. "I'm here as a representative of Butler, Mitchener, and Holmes, attorneys specializing in player trades, agents, and the politics and the business of hockey. I have been asked by your brother to put certain things in place, and I'm here to talk you through them, and also to answer any questions you might have." He paused.

I think he wanted me to say something but I was stuck on the fact that his white hair was sticking up at the back, and also that he was a hockey attorney. What skater even had that kind of thing?

"Miles has the paperwork for you to sign for the money I'm using to clear the debtors that—"

"Hell no," I stood so fast my chair rattled and my head swam. "I said I didn't want your money—"

"Sit down!" Dan shouted in my face, and fuck me if that worked as a charm and I slunk down into my chair. "You *will* sign these papers, Henry. You will agree to my help, we will get this fixed, and then you will get back on the ice. Are we done messing around now?"

He was flushed, and I wondered if it was as hard for him as it was for me to be sitting here doing this. Miles cleared his throat, and slid over a piece of thick paper with his company heading that held a simple statement of six names, plus a row of figures. I read them once, and the total at the bottom, and then read them again. "What is this?" In my heart I already knew what it was and I felt sick.

"A summary of your creditors," Miles offered gently, "and the current outstanding debts up until close of business today."

I went down the numbers again, but they were so big that my eyes blurred and I wasn't sure if it was because of tears, or my bad eye shutting down. "Three million, more than that, nearly three and half million dollars? I haven't earned anywhere near that, how did Ed and Mom… how did they…?"

Miles slid another piece of paper over to me, and it was full of legal jargon, and right at the bottom was my signature, and next to it what appeared to be Dan's name. I'd seen his autograph before on the times when I used to check up on him, and this didn't look very much like his signature at all.

"They faked it, Henry, when I signed my last contract with Philadelphia, eight million, and it looks as if Ed persuaded these investors that I was backing the scheme he was part of. This is my problem too, but it wouldn't stand in court, this isn't my signature." He pointed at the bottom. "Is that yours?"

My blurry eyesight wouldn't cooperate, but by sheer will I managed to focus on the tiny writing, and it certainly looked like mine, although I didn't recognize the form. Why had I signed what the lawyer handed to me, why hadn't I questioned the spaces next to my name, why had I trusted Mom? I was dead inside, lost, and even when Dan scooted around to sit next to me, I didn't feel anything but alone. I'd loved my mom, trusted her, and look what she'd done to me. I'd trusted and thought I'd loved Aarni, and what had happened there. What kind of man was I not to see these things?

Miles began to talk again. "I've arranged a transfer of three-point-seven-four million to the creditors, this coming from Daniel Greenaway to clear all debts accrued under this contract." The third piece of paper slid over, and this time it was a clearer sheet, authorizing the transfer and signed by Dan, and then farther down a note that this was not a loan, but a discharge of family debts.

"I can't sign this; do you even have this much money? Jesus Christ, Dan."

"Let's do this," Dan murmured, "I'm on six mill a year right now, let this go, pay everyone off. Then we just have Mom to deal with, and we can do that together."

"I can't ask you to do this."

Miles stood and cleared his throat. "I'll give you a moment."

Only when I was sure Miles was gone, did I turn to Dan and lose my shit. I'm not sure if it was crying, or pleading, or just a plain old meltdown, but he pulled me in for a hug, and held me close for the longest time. I felt safe there in my brother's arms, and he was chatting away in my ear about family, and Mom, and brother stuff, until I started to believe it when he was saying everything would be okay. When I'd signed the paper I felt the weight of obligation, but it was balanced by a fragile peace of knowing I didn't owe any money.

"Love you, little brother," he murmured in my ear as we hugged goodbye, and then, in a daze I watched them both leave, Miles in his Mercedes, Dan in his Porsche.

"Are you okay?" Apollo asked as he handed me a drink. It was pink, fizzy, and decorated with pineapple and a tiny umbrella. The drink made me smile, Apollo made me smile, and my brother was my brother again. Even my headache had gone. I wanted to tell him what had just happened, because it was Mom, and money, and my brother, and it was too important to keep to myself. Only... was it too much to burden him with? Was it right to expect him to understand? Would he even begin to see what I'd done in my stupidity? So instead I avoided talking about it at all.

"Yeah, just some family legal stuff."

Apollo gave me a smile, and I loved that smile, then he pirouetted in front of me before planting a kiss on my lips and dancing away. "Come on, big guy. Ryker and Jacob will be here in thirty and I need your help getting something from the top cabinet." He headed to the kitchen and I followed.

Because now, I was hungry for more kisses.

R YKER BEGAN TALKING EVEN BEFORE HE AND J ACOB GOT into the house proper. Jacob was the one to deal with locking the car, fetching their contributions for dinner, and chatting to Apollo. Me? I was hearing first-hand about how Ryker was *really* feeling about the news of Tate joining us, and he hadn't stopped for a breath yet.

"Then Dad said it would be like Pittsburgh, right, how we'd have two lines centered with top line centers to split the opposition's defense, and all I could think was that I was proud he thought I was that good, and pissed that I'm sure I will be second line. But then Ten said it was all about the Cup and the team, and a strong team is a joy to be part of, and then he started talking about when he played with Tate and how he understood how I felt and—"

Apollo stood between us, but Ryker and I were taller, so he began to jump up and down. At first Ryker kept talking, leaning around my leaping Latino, but then he got the message, about the same time as Apollo stopped jumping. Jacob snorted with laughter, and then Apollo placed his hand on Ryker's chest and shoved him back until he was by the sofa, and then with one final push Ryker was sitting next to Jacob. Just this action seemed to reset Ryker who was much calmer as he sipped another of the fruity drinks and talked much more rationally.

Somehow between Ryker talking, Jacob placating, Apollo feeding us, and eating, we hadn't talked about how I felt Tate would fit into the team. I could see that single moment when Ryker realized he had monopolized the conversation, and he flushed scarlet when Jacob elbowed him to remind him he hadn't asked me a single thing.

"My bad," Ryker fist bumped me, and I didn't care he hadn't asked me about Tate, because that was far down on my list after recovery, rehab, and the confusion that was my feelings for Apollo.

"How are you doing, Henry?" Jacob asked and side-eyed Ryker.

"I'm doing okay, working on drills, need to get on the ice if you're up for it, Ry?"

"Always," Ryker agreed immediately.

And then, as if I had no control over my mouth-brain connection, my carefully constructed wall collapsed in an instant. "Also my mom and this guy bankrupted me, and left me over three million in debt, and my brother is funding the repayment of the debt, and I'm pretty much screwed financially, but that's okay, because when I'm back on the team it'll all be golden." God knows why I blurted that out.

Next to me, Apollo stiffened. "She did? Who's the guy? He is?"

I knew I should have told him sooner, after all we'd had sex, right? I owed him some part of me that others didn't see, the vulnerable underbelly that you only show the people you get close to. I rationalized that I hadn't told him because we'd been fixing dinner, or that I was still in shock, or that Ryker was coming, or even that I had Tate to think about, but I'd forgotten Apollo. I knew the reveal would go no farther than this room, because I trusted Ryker, and with Ryker came Jacob, and they were the best couple I'd ever seen. I trusted Apollo because…

He's been hired to help you. He's contracted to keep confidences.

None of that sat right in my head, but there had to be a reason I dropped the news when I was certain it wasn't just me and Apollo? Did that prove I didn't love him? Or was I just lost in the feeling that I didn't deserve to love him? Did I even know what love was?

Apollo was quiet as Jacob asked me questions about what had happened, and the whole sorry mess slipped out in gentle explanations. Ryker and Jacob hugged me hard when they left, both assuring me that I was going to be okay, and then I went to find Apollo, who was rummaging in the kitchen and tidying things away.

"Ryker seems okay with the news," Apollo began brightly, "About Tate, I mean, after I jumped up and down like a jack-in-a-box to stop him shouting in your face about every single conversation he'd had since he'd found out."

"Apollo—"

"And did you see the way Jacob held his hand all through it, as if by sheer will alone he could get Ryker to calm down."

"Can we—?"

"Will you help me put the spices back on the top shelf? Otherwise I'll need to get the stool out again, and last time it got wedged under the counter and was difficult to get out."

"Stop." It was my turn to talk, and I had a lot I needed to say to him. I scooped him up and set him on the counter, standing between his legs and pinning him there. "I'm sorry I didn't tell you what Dan was here for," I whispered against his cheek, and waited for him to get angry.

"It's okay." He put his hands on my shoulders and eased away from me. "You don't have to share anything with me right now. I'm just the person here to—"

"Don't say that. You're not *just* anything to me." I kissed him, and poured every apology and ounce of messed up emotion into the kiss. At first he tried to move back, and then the passion became more, and the kiss deepened, and he stopped fighting, his hands snaking around my neck.

I regretted not telling him every secret I'd ever held, I wished I'd confided in him to show how much he meant to me.

I'm so stupid.

And when Apollo went home, I would never have confronted how I felt, and worse, I would never have considered whether or not I could truly love someone again.

ELEVEN

Apollo

By the time the Stanley Cup finals had rolled around in early June, I'd gotten a firm handle on my emotions. Not really. I spent a lot of time hiding in my bedroom cursing my stupid heart and whimpering into the pillows while "Who's That Girl" played on a loop all night long. I spoke to Adler as often as possible, but given he and the Railers were in the finals against a tough San Diego Swarm team, our chatting was at a minimum. Not that I would have told him anyway. Falling for Henry was not something to wave around despite what Tía Sofía had said. No, there was no sense in throwing myself at Henry emotionally. Physically, I tried to keep my distance, honestly, I did. But a week would go by and he'd kiss my ear or compliment my ankle or buy me a new bangle and I'd find my heart overflowing with emotion. Those emotions, it seemed, ran right to my dick. Two hard dicks in the same room always ended up with my heels to Jesus. I was such a little slut…

So, instead of acting on my feelings for a man who

didn't love me back, I threw myself into being the best companion in Arizona. Which translated to fussing over Henry and throwing parties. We had people over all the time, for any reason at all. Most of the team had gone, Alex and Seb were in the UK, Vlad was in Russia, and Colorado and the Chaotic Furballs were touring up and down the West coast. During a long night with Madonna and my buried affections, I came up with a marvelous idea. Today that idea was coming to life and it was a grand thing if I did say so myself.

"Tell me again why you've had artificial ice laid down inside the ballroom," Tía Sofía said as we stood at the doorway of the massive room while Henry did laps on the synthetic ice.

"Because it's a viewing party for game seven of the Cup finals!"

She stared down at me as if I'd lost all reason. "If you say so. Personally, a buffet for the guests and a big screen TV would have been enough, but who am I to say? Obviously you're not using these outlandish soirees to hide your feelings as we've discussed about four thousand times in the past few weeks now, are you? Silly me. Old Aunty Sofía, what do *I* know about love and romance? Pish-posh. Go home you old bitty, you're drunk."

I ignored her. It wasn't easy to ignore a six-foot-two woman in a Tennant Rowe-Madsen jersey, black leggings, and sparkly silver strappy sandals which I wished I owned, but I did manage to ignore. Somewhat. Not at all.

"I'm not using anything for anything. Just hush." With that I stalked away to check on the food and look up where to buy strappy silver sandals online. Henry liked the fake ice idea when I'd shown it to him. That was all that mattered. Making him as happy as I could while I was here. The doorbell rang. I heard Tía Sofía rushing to answer it.

I met the first guests with a smile and a tray of cocktails. Mark Westman-Reid and Coach Rowen Carmichael both seemed rather lost but took the margaritas I'd offered them with awkward smiles. I knew that the head coach didn't do player parties often, but the players in the area were scarce so I'd had to dip into the coaching staff, management, and owners.

"This is quite the house," Rowen said, taking a sip of his cocktail. "And your aunt is quite the hostess." Tía Sofía had Mark by the arm, dragging him around to see the rest of the Lockhart manse. I smiled widely, leading him to the ballroom. His eyes flared. "Wow," he muttered, with salt stuck to his lips.

"Hey, Coach!" Henry yelled as he made another lap, his skates gliding over the synthetic ice as if it were the real stuff. "Did you bring your skates?"

"I uhm… no. Sorry. I thought that was a misprint on the invitations," Rowen replied.

"It's amazing, isn't it? I wanted to set up an outdoor rink by the pool but it's been a hundred and four for a week, so we went with this instead!" I bounced around, the cocktails sloshing a bit on the silver tray. "We have things ready in the entertainment room. The food will be out shortly! Just follow that towering Latina in the Tennant Rowe jersey and—"

The doorbell rang. Tía Sofía skittered past the open double doors. I smiled at Henry as he skated by, a puck on his stick. Ryker and Jacob appeared behind me, and that was that. They rubbed my head in thanks, sat down, and skated up.

I wandered off to serve drinks then haul the ribs, chicken wings, chili, and other sporty foods into the TV room. We ended up with about twenty people, six of them were Westman-Reids who probably felt compelled to reply an invitation with the name Lockhart on it. We settled in to watch game seven, most of us in Railers dusky blue, but a few were sporting the teal and white of the Swarm.

By the end of that game, the two in the Swarm jerseys were celebrating. Those of us in dusky blue were stunned. The Railers had lost by one goal. It hurt me down deep in my soul. Those men were like family to me. Adler was my brother from another mother. The camera panning over their dejected faces and Stan kneeling in his crease with the puck that had slid past him still sitting in the net about broke my heart. I ran out of the TV room to wail in the kitchen.

"Hey, are you okay?" I spun around to hide my face from Henry when he appeared.

"I'm fine, just disappointed. Did you see Adler's face?"

Henry slipped his arms around me from behind, kissed my neck, and held me tight. I melted back into him, tears sneaking down my cheeks.

"You're so empathic, so giving, so in tune with everyone else. I love that about you."

I knew his words were meant as comfort and praise, but they only added to my misery. He loved my giving heart but not me. I wiggled out of his arms and stepped away, not wanting to be held by him right now, because everything was a confused mess. He looked hurt, his expression normally enough for me to rush back to touch him, reassure him, but the shock at the Railers loss, and my compassion for Adler, made me want to be alone.

"I'm being a ninny." I coughed as I hurried to the sink to splash cold water on my face. "It's only a hockey game. And we have guests." Dabbing at my wet cheeks with a dish towel with chickens on it—a funny joke present from Alex who enjoyed pointing out that the Spanish name for a chicken was *pollo* which was super close to Apollo—then plastered on a smile. "Go back and tend to the guests, please? I'll bring out some sweets in a minute." I couldn't look at him, because I knew he'd still have that confused expression and what did he have to be confused about? He wasn't in love with me; he didn't understand what love was like.

"Are you sure you're okay?" He padded over to touch my cheek. I nearly lost it again but I sniffled and nodded and forced a grin.

"Yes. I'll call Adler before I go to bed."

He leaned in to brush a kiss to my cheek which I avoided, and with a soft sigh he ambled off to play the host. Shaking and sniveling, I managed to get the cookies and tarts I'd baked onto a platter and carried it to the guests. The party kind of fizzled out after the sweets and coffee, with Henry and me on opposite sides of the room. I could see that a couple of times he wanted to talk to me, but I changed the subject or spoke to someone else. In fact, I had a less than riveting discussion with Mark about this year's fashions just so I didn't have to talk to Henry, and I could see Henry's frustration growing. Finally, Tía Sofía, Henry, and I stood by the front door to say goodbye to everyone.

"You need to switch to waterproof mascara, baby," Tía Sofía whispered as we waved at our departing guests winding down the serpentine driveway.

"I didn't plan on crying. I thought we'd win," I replied as the last taillights disappeared from view. Henry turned away from us and went inside without saying goodnight to my aunt. That was highly rude and out of character for him. "I'm sorry he didn't say goodbye. Maybe he has a headache."

"It's fine. It takes more than a tiny little snub to get my panties in a wad. Kiss me goodnight, *mijo.*" She bent down and I bussed both her cheeks then walked her to her red Jag parked in the shadows of the mansion. "Apollo, do me a favor. Talk to Henry. Tell him how you feel."

I nodded.

She sighed, knowing I probably wasn't going to do what she asked of me. With a roll of her beautiful brown eyes, she folded herself behind the wheel, put the roof down, tied a white scarf around her head, and sped off into the desert night.

I wandered the backyard looking for Henry. He was seated on the edge of the pool soaking his feet. The night was thick with insect song. He glanced up at me as I approached and I could see that confusion had turned to annoyance, and he was spoiling for a fight. The telltale signs of a headache bracketed his eyes, and he pressed his fingers to his temples and winced even as he spoke.

"You said 'we'," he said.

"'We', what?"

"You said you though that *we'd win* when you were talking about the Railers. I thought maybe the Raptors were your team now, as they're mine, but I can see where your loyalties lie."

My mouth dropped open. Was he really mad that I was still a fan of the Railers? Did he really want to fight tonight? What did he expect? It wasn't as if we were anything real, and yet again I was defaulting to a relationship where I *knew* I was loved.

"My loyalties are to the man who I grew up with. Adler's like a brother to me—"

"Yeah, I know what Adler is to you. Good thing you get to go back to him soon."

"What are you doing?" I asked.

"Finally knowing for sure where I fit in!"

With that he rose and stormed off, his fists clenched, his wet feet slapping the cement, and his shoulders tight. I thought to run after him and demand an apology and an explanation. What did he care what went down with me and Adler? Henry wasn't in love with me, had never once declared any kind of wish to be committed to me and only me. Ugh. Ugh. *Ugh.*

Love was shit. Why did I keep doing it? I thundered inside to clean up. The sight of the mounds of dirty dishes, flatware, and glasses made me groan, but I dove in, knowing it would help get my mind off the sadness of the loss.

Two hours later, way past midnight, I crept past Henry's door. He might have still been angry, or in pain, but I'd gotten over my anger an hour ago. Now I just wanted to make up and have him love me until dawn broke. The pull to join him was strong, but I'd kept that one barrier between us. If I woke in his arms, there would be no way I'd leave here in September without being smashed into bits. As it was, my departure was going to be brutal. The big house was silent aside from the AC blowing and making a small wind chime in the solarium sing out. I stripped and showered, eager to get the sweat and stink of cooking fumes off me. Wearing nothing but a silky robe, I hustled to my bed.

My bed was too big, too cold, and too empty but I climbed into it anyway, my phone in hand, I dialed Adler. I was only an hour ahead of him in San Diego and knew he'd be up reliving the night, the mistakes he thought he'd made, the plays that could've worked better, the fates themselves probably. He answered on the first ring.

"Hey," I said, slipping my feet under the thick covers then tugging them to my chest. "I'm so sorry about the loss. You guys gave it your all."

"Hey." He sighed. My heart ached. "Thanks for the call. I fucking miss the shit out of you, Apollo."

"I miss you too. Do you want to talk?"

"About the game tonight? No, I really don't. I fucked up. That giveaway in the first period was unforgivable. They should trade my stupid ass."

"Stop. Just stop. A team wins and loses as a whole. Everyone made mistakes. Tennant pulling that tripping penalty in the second period, Eric whiffing on that penalty shot, and Stan letting in that soft goal at the end of the game."

"Not his fault. He's been playing with a groin injury

the past week. That was on us and the defense. We should have had that crease covered better."

I closed my eyes and counted to twenty. This was typical. I suspected every man on the Railers was raking himself over the coals for choking in the final game. None of them would be proud of themselves for making it that far, they'd just beat themselves up for not bringing the Cup back to Harrisburg.

"Why don't you stop by for a visit before you go home. Is Layton with you?"

"He is, yeah."

"Then stop. It's been months since we saw each other. I mean, it's your house after all, come spend some time here. I'll make you cookies."

"Those ones with the lime and guava filling?"

That made me smile. "Yep. A whole batch. You'll have to fight Henry for them though."

"Okay, yeah, I'd like that. No need to go home right away and see the looks of disgust on the fans' faces. I'll let you know when we leave. Hey, man, thanks for the invite. Spending time with you will really help. I love you, bro."

"I love you too, Adler. See you tomorrow." I hung up, swiped at my eyes, and snuggled down into the covers, wondering why it was that the wrong man had just said he loved me and the right man was in his room mad at me.

ADLER ARRIVED AT NOON THE NEXT DAY, LAYTON AT HIS side. Henry had opted out of speaking to me all morning, moving around the house like a ghost, and had just now shown his face to welcome Adler. I, being a rather bitchy thing when someone was on my shit-list, gave Henry the cold shoulder as the blue Corvette roared up to the house and Adler unfolded his long legs from behind the wheel.

I nearly killed myself darting out to greet him. He scooped me up as if I were a ragdoll, hugged me tight, and kissed my head a few dozen times before setting me down to give me a good, long look.

"You look good. Tanned, smiling, and pretty as a picture. Henry! Hey, man." Adler charged up to Henry, slapped him on the shoulder, hugged him, patted his head, and then dragged him inside as he rambled on about hockey. I walked over to Layton lifting bags from the rear of the car.

"Need help?" I asked after giving him a short hug.

"No thanks, we packed light so that Adler could take us shopping for clothes when we ran out. I was too tired to argue." He shouldered both big bags then slammed the trunk shut. "You look good. He's been talking about seeing you nonstop. This was an excellent idea. Thanks for suggesting it."

"Well, it's a treat for me too. I miss him a lot. I am sorry about the Railers."

"We are too but there's always next season. The Swarm earned that Cup win." We walked into the house and followed the sounds of two grown men slipping around on synthetic ice.

"Holy shit, this is amazing!" Adler hooted as he scurried across the room in his stocking feet. "Foxy Man, we so need some of this at our place!"

"Yep, that's just what we need at our place," Layton whispered.

I nudged him along, my sight skipping over Henry staring at me from the other side of the ice. The company who put it down would be here tomorrow to clean it up so he might as well enjoy it now. Not that he was enjoying it by the looks, more intent on staring at me as if I'd stolen his stick or something. Ugh. Feelings. Ugh. Romance. Ugh. Men.

The rest of the day flew by once Adler got off the fake ice. We four lounged by the pool most of the day, eating and talking hockey and movies and music. In honor of Adler being here I'd allowed the music playing through the house to be 80s Hair Bands. Night fell over the desert city, and we'd done nothing but swim and eat and catch up. It felt as if we'd been apart forever, not just a few months.

"… longest we've ever been separated," Adler said as he and I lay on inflatable rafts in the pool under a million stars. "This place rocks. Why don't I spend more time here?"

"Because Layton is in Harrisburg."

"True that."

He paddled around me in lazy circles. Layton and Henry had gone to bed two hours ago, Layton claiming fatigue and Henry stating he had a headache. I'd stop by his room on my way to bed to check on him. Just because he was acting weird with me and Adler didn't mean I wasn't worried about him. What if his concussion was making him sick suddenly? Or his eye was putting pressure on his brain? Oh shit. I was a terrible companion to not talk to him all day!

"… a word I've said the past five minutes?"

"What? I who? Yes, of course I heard. I have to check on Henry. I think his brain is pressured."

Whatever Adler called to me I blocked out as I ran inside, water trailing behind me, as I raced to Henry's door and knocked on it. When he answered a minute or two later, looking rumpled from sleep, I nearly leapt into the air in relief.

He gave me a quick once-over. "You're making puddles on the floor."

"I'll mop it up later." I pulled up my sodden trunks. "I was worried about your head. Does it still hurt? Should we maybe call the doctor? It's been a day-long headache and—"

"I'm okay." I folded my arms over my chest. "Really, I'm okay. The headache is not really bad at all. I'm just not handling seeing you and Adler together. I know it's selfish and stupid." He pressed his temples again, and I knew he was struggling. "I was used to being the only man you fretted over and now that he's here it's—"

I tossed myself at him, climbing up over him like he was the world's sexiest jungle gym. He cupped my ass as my mouth found his. I wound around him, and we kissed like lovers who'd been apart for eons. I carded my fingers into his hair, cementing his mouth to mine.

"Get a room," Adler tossed out as he strolled by on his way to the mauve guest room. Henry nearly dropped me to my ass. I caught myself on the doorjamb, threw a glower at Adler, and then looked up at Henry's sweet, sweet face. The door down the hall clicked shut.

"You're the only man I'm interested in fretting over in that way," I whispered to Henry, rising to my soggy toes to steal another kiss. "Adler is my brother, you're my lover."

He bent down to lick at my mouth. "I'm not even jealous of Adler, or any of it... I'm a mess. Please come inside. I really want to love you tonight. Let me make up for being such a stupid dick all day."

It was tempting. *So* fucking tempting. But if I stepped over that threshold there would be no turning back. Every tiny atom of my being would be left behind when I went north. I had to hold onto something when it was time to go, even if it was a minuscule sprinkle of Apollo essence, I had to keep that for me.

"I can't. You know how loud I am. They'll hear us." I patted his scruffy cheek then made the long walk to my room, where I hurried to get inside before my resolve melted away like ice under a hot sun.

Adler and Layton stayed for a week. The four of us spent all that time together, even going with Henry to his rehab appointments. We went to the desert, hiked the mountains, we went to the Grand Canyon, Monument Valley, and the Petrified Forest. We played golf, waterskied, and took a rafting trip down the Colorado River. We went to Seattle for two days to see Colorado and the Chaotic Furballs play in a bar that Layton and I felt should have been condemned. It took my ears two days to recover from the metal music, and Henry ended up with yet another headache caused by the walls of pulsating speakers. The band had an after-party which we'd been invited to attend but turned down once we saw that it was on the tour bus. One look into that den of carnal pleasures had Henry's face turning bright red and Layton's cheeks flaming.

When it was time for them to leave, I cried a little when I was hugging Adler goodbye.

"I'll see you in September," I told Adler. He glanced from me to Henry helping Layton fit the bag into the Corvette's trunk, smiled, and then chucked my chin.

"Yeah, okay, if you say so. Take care of him."

"I will, you know that."

"Yeah I do. Love you, man."

They pulled away, the tires spewing dust into the heated air. Henry wrapped his arms around me, lifting me from the ground as I yelped in shock.

"They're gone now. You can be as loud as you want."

"What are you waiting for? Get me inside fast!" I said with a laugh.

He carried me inside, laid me down on the nearest thing with a cushion which happened to be a bench just inside the foyer, and proceeded to make me fill the house with cries of passion.

TWELVE

Henry

"I'M SEEING A LOT OF IMPROVEMENT." DOCTOR SYKES stepped away from me, dropping the tiny magnifying flashlight to his desk and marking something in his notes.

I reached for Apollo's hand. He took it and held tight. "And that's a good thing?" I hoped the Doc would nod, and we'd be done. I didn't want him to qualify his statement with yet more delays and warnings, because training camp was in three days and I was determined to be back on the ice. I'd been training with Ryker and Alex, and my senses had gone from middling to intense. I'd slipped into a skating relationship with both of them on the ice that wouldn't continue when Jens was back from vacation, but I knew I was achieving on the ice, and that had to be a good thing.

"Can I ask about the headaches?" he asked instead, and I could have screamed, but I didn't because this was a ten thousand dollar appointment and even the air in this room was probably charged for by the hour. It was one room in a suite of rooms just for Doctor Sykes, who was the best of the best, or so the team had assured me. They had a vested interest in getting me better now they'd decided I was worth fixing.

"The last headache was a few months ago now," I replied. Right after my post-Stanley Cup final meltdown. Apollo and I had found ways of alleviating the tension in my neck, which we both thought was causing the worst of them. He'd read up on manipulation of the muscle attachments to the skull, and I swear my headaches eased in days, and hadn't returned yet. The fact that they didn't seem to be connected to my eye issue was a positive step in the right direction, but that didn't mean I didn't have the eye injury to worry about as a whole.

"Okay, then," Doc signed a piece of paper with a flourish, then closed the buff folder. "Consider yourself officially discharged."

"Huh?" *Brilliant use of language there.* "I don't have to come back? Is there nothing you can do? Am I done being a hockey player—?"

Apollo squeezed my hand very hard, so hard that it snapped me out of my thoughts and then I caught the Doctor Sykes' smile.

"No, I'm discharging you because you're as good as you can be, and that is better than we ever expected. You'll *never* regain that part of the peripheral vision you lost, but the swelling is gone, the floaters are less, and as far as I'm concerned, you're cleared to play. If that is for the Raptors, or any other professional team, then I want to see you every other month. On the other hand, if you decide you want to *retire* at this point and take up a career as a coach or work behind a desk, then we can push the appointments to twice a year."

"Thank you." Those two words didn't seem like enough to say to a doctor, for the way he'd explained my options in language even I could understand, and the way he'd cared for me since the first referral.

He leaned forward and laced his fingers together, resting his hands on the desk. "What will you do?"

I exchanged glances with Apollo but his expression was carefully neutral. What did I want to do? What should I do? What did others want me to do?

Make decisions for yourself right now, so that maybe one day you can move on to bigger and better things.

"I'm going to training camp," I announced. "I'm getting my place back on the team, and then I'm restarting my life."

Doctor Sykes nodded. "You're just like every professional athlete in his prime who has sat there and said the same thing." We shook hands, took an appointment card from the wonderful lady at reception, and with a rising energy that couldn't be contained, I tugged Apollo out of the building, and as soon as we were outside I let out a whoop of joy, scooped him into my arms and swung him around in a huge circle. He was smiling, and laughing, and on the steps by the car I kissed him soundly.

The best news in the world and I was sharing it with the man I—

Loved? Was this what love was? This desperate need to share every emotion inside me with Apollo?

"Let me down, you big lug!" Apollo ordered with a grin.

I groaned when he slid down me to stand on his own. I didn't want him to leave my arms, I wanted to hold him forever.

Fuck. This could be…

By the time we made it home I had a mental list of people to call. Coach, Ryker, I needed to find a new agent to take me to the next level, but first I needed to talk to Dan. Apollo made drinks, and bustled around the kitchen. I called my brother who answered on the third ring and sounded like he'd run for the phone.

"What's wrong?" he asked immediately.

I heard someone murmuring words behind him. I'd yet to meet his girlfriend, Anna, but she was a TV star in Sweden and wasn't over Stateside much. Given that fact, this was probably why he was out of breath because he was making up for lost time, and I felt guilty at what I might have interrupted.

"Nothing's wrong, sorry to call, but I've got the all clear. I'm okay to get to training camp in August. I'm fucking okay!"

"Oh shit, Jesus, kid, that's amazing. That's the best news, Henry." More murmuring. "Okay, I'll tell him, yeah. Anna says hi and well done. Yeah, I know he's not a kid," he added, clearly talking to Anna, "but he's my little brother, so I get to call him that."

I was ridiculously happy with the call. "Say hi back to her, tell her I want to meet her soon and we can celebrate, and oh God, I just realized, if I get a decent contract I can start to pay you back."

"Henry—"

"No, Dan, let me have this."

"Okay, okay, we'll talk about it later and—"

"I'm not arguing. Now I'm going to kiss Apollo and eat cookies. Later!"

We said our goodbyes, and I twirled Apollo again, pressing him up on the counter and standing between his legs. The words were right there on my tongue, *I love you, I'm not sure what love is for real, but you make me better, you are my life, please don't leave.*

Then inevitably the negative thoughts spiraled, because I couldn't bring myself to say anything like that. *He must be so tired of waiting for me, why is he still here? I need to tell him how I feel.*

I wish I could tell him, but that part of me which needed to commit to how I felt was broken. Was it my heart? Or my head? All I knew was that the fragile need inside me to tell him how I was feeling was stuck, and I couldn't commit to saying the words.

"I'm so pleased for you," Apollo said brightly, and twisted his hands together behind my neck. "It's time for you to take the next step."

We made out for the longest time, until he slipped away, talking about chocolate, and baking, and tins, and all I could think was that he sensed that broken part of me, and that he was going to pull away now.

Probably what I deserve.

Lorraine sat back in her chair, looking just this side of smug. "Told you," she crowed, and high-fived me. "That's the best news," she added, and then indicated I take a seat in the large room. I sank into the stuffed sofa and folded my hands in my lap, waiting until she was sitting before allowing the floodgates to open. God knows how I'd kept everything in this long, given it had been an entire twenty-four hours of tiptoeing around the house avoiding Apollo because I didn't know how to handle the feelings in my head, and the ache in my heart.

"I called you because I need some of the other stuff you said you did, the talking thing."

She tilted her head. "Okay, shoot."

I opened my mouth to talk, and the words dried up. "Shit," I couldn't believe that everything I had in my head was refusing to turn into words. "I see a counselor, and I can talk to him, but sitting here I don't know what the hell to say."

"You realize we've talked every training session we've had? Do you recall that time you fell over the medicine ball, and you wouldn't get up and we talked about the mountains you have to climb?"

"You said that sometimes it was okay to stay at base camp," I murmured. "But that sometimes the view from the top is worth the climb, and I needed to make a decision if I wanted the beauty of up high, or…"

"Whether you want the safety of base camp. See? Every moment I've been with you we've been talking about your career, assessing the needs you have, working on your mental health."

"I didn't even realize," I admitted, and then waved at the room. "So why in here today?"

"Because you sounded like you needed to talk without me using mountain metaphors. So, why did you call?"

I thought back to the moment when I'd caught Apollo shimmying to a Madonna song in the kitchen, shaking his hips and waving his hands dramatically. It had been funny, and sweet, and I'd been overwhelmed with *something.*

"My ex, Aarni, he was controlling." No, that wasn't right to start there. I needed to go back farther than that. I wriggled lower on the sofa; the weight of everything I had to get off my chest was pushing me down. Or maybe I was half hoping the thing would swallow me whole. "I have to start way back, is that okay?"

"Always."

"My dad died when I was ten, it was sudden, a heart attack, one day he was there, the next he was gone. Same as my brother Dan, one day he was at home hugging me and telling me everything was going to be okay, the next he was drafted and on his way to Denver, then Philly. Mom became controlling, of me that is, not herself. She had boyfriends, and they were all going to be my new dad, and I ignored what she said. No one was going to replace Dad, and no amount of step-brothers would replace Dan." I paused and glanced up to see Lorraine nodding. "Am I making sense? Do I need to go back even further?"

"If you think you need to."

I shook my head furiously. "No, I'm good. So, the thing is, Mom met this guy, Ed. He seemed like a good man to start with. I mean he made Mom happy, but when she wasn't around, he would tell me I was messing up all the time. Not just that I didn't practice enough, or that I wasn't as good as Dan, or that I needed to work harder. He would imply things in a much subtler way, manipulating me."

"Gaslighting?"

"Yeah, I guess you could call it that. It was my fault that him and my mom were arguing, or that he had to hold down a shitty job in a convenience store to feed us. It was my fault that Dan had gone away, and that he didn't send home enough money. And I listened to him, and when Mom didn't back me up, I took every part of what he said seriously. I mean, I was only ten when Dan left, and he had this whole new life, and he didn't want his kid brother around him, or at least that is what Ed told me. He didn't want me talking to Dan about what was happening, and it's only with hindsight that I see that."

"How did Ed stop you talking to Dan?"

"I don't know, genuinely. Then there was the money. Ed wrote letters to Dan asking for money, explaining that it was Dan's job to send us what we needed, and then he got me to sign them. He made me feel as if Dan owed me, and I still don't know how Ed managed to get inside my head, but mom never stopped it, and it destroyed my relationship with Dan."

"Knowing that you were manipulated is very insightful," she murmured.

"It doesn't make it right."

"No, but it's a step in the right direction. You can blame yourself for it all, but if there is a kernel of understanding how you got to this position, then it's a start. Have you talked to your brother?"

"Yes. Yeah, I have. He visited me in the hospital, and then he tried to keep in touch after that, but I pushed him away. Mom was so broken over what happened to me, and I just wanted to keep everyone happy. But when her and

Ed took everything from me..." I huffed noisily, not sure how to explain without sounding like the fucking idiot I'd been

"Took everything how? Emotionally?"

"Well yeah, I guess so, but they also took all my money, left me owing millions, because I was stupid enough to believe that despite being with Ed, Mom loved me and was strong enough to look out for me."

"You weren't stupid." Lorraine shook her head. "He was manipulating you, and you had no choice. He sabotaged your self-esteem, made you feel small, devalued you, and it seems to me he's an expert at playing the game. Have you considered that your mom was a victim as much as you," She stopped for a moment, sipping her water, and continued. "Tell me something honest, Henry."

"Like what?"

"How do you feel when I tell you that it wasn't your fault? Are you defensive of Ed?"

"No, God no."

"Your mom?"

I don't know. "Maybe."

"And your brother? How do you feel about his part in this? Surely he could have forced his way through the defenses you put up and come back to you."

"No, you see he couldn't, I know that for a fact, because I told him to stay away, and he loved me, and listened to me, and thought he was doing the best thing."

"So this somehow leads to your ex?"

I couldn't help shuddering at the thought of Aarni and what he'd done, and of that damn blog he'd written that had been nothing more than a weave of lies. The amount of times I'd sat at my laptop and started writing the real story, but it had always spilled out in words dripping with acid and I never saved any of it. Apollo said I was self-soothing, and he probably had a point. My counselor said I was doing well getting it out of me, but it was something else that Lorraine had said to me that was the reason I was here now.

"To cut a long story short, he was filling a void in me and I let him hurt me."

"I'm sorry," Lorraine murmured, and I nodded to indicate I'd heard her.

"That's an aside," I didn't really want to talk about Aarni, I wanted to talk hockey which was my safe place. "The reason I wanted to talk to you, was something else you said last week. It wasn't a mountain analogy, but you joked about how I must love hockey so much to want to put all this work in."

She laughed then, "Hockey is in your blood and it defines you right now. The reason you've been here nearly every day working with me is because your love for hockey is more that the hate you have of some of the things I asked you to do."

"Like the wall climb thing, I hated the height of that."

"But you did it, twice, and then you broke the record for the fastest climb just to prove you could. So love for hockey wins over fear." She laughed at her own words. "That sounds so corny."

Abruptly, a curtain in my head parted, light spilling through as if I'd had an epiphany. Was it possible that everything I was fighting in my head about my feelings for Apollo, all the barriers and the noes, was because I actually did love him but that I hadn't worked through enough pain to get to the end of the journey?

When I left Lorraine my head was spinning, and Apollo beaming at me from the driver seat made it worse. I kissed him hard, ignored my tortured thoughts, then buckled up.

"Good workout?" he asked when we separated. He hadn't balked at me saying that I was going in on my own, in fact he'd settled down with his Kindle and a travel mug of coffee and waved me off. He was always there for me, whatever I needed. *Anything.*

"Yeah, good."

"So, rink next?"

I had practice today, some of the guys who'd come back from vacation or the various specialist camps would be there, and I wanted to soak up the camaraderie and the pranks and the stupid jokes. The ice. Skating. I needed that because I loved it, because it was part of me, and nothing would stop me from pushing myself for the thing I loved.

Apollo turned up the music, singing along as we made our way back into Tucson. I closed my eyes and let my thoughts wander. I knew I didn't love Aarni and never would. I didn't love Mom but there was a biological link that meant one day I could possibly love her again. *Yeah, right, like maybe when hell freezes over.* I knew *for sure* I loved Dan, but he was my brother and that was a genetic connection, right? So if I knew who I was and wasn't capable of loving, then why did I feel so reluctant to share any of this with Apollo?

Because I need to be stronger. Someone like him could

make me vulnerable again. Or maybe because I'd be opening my heart to hurt?

The parking lot for the practice arena was fuller than usual and I recognized some of the cars, grinning with excitement as I walked in past security and finally reached the locker rooms. Apollo went straight to the seats to watch, and I suited up, exchanging banter with some of the guys, until the room went silent. I looked in the direction people were staring, and saw why everyone had stopped talking.

"Hi," the gorgeous man with dark hair said from the door. "Tate Collins," he added unnecessarily, and stepped into the room.

For a moment everyone stayed silent, and then a few of the team went up to say hello; Ryker, Alex, led by Vlad whose booming voice rose over the welcomes. Some of the team didn't move, the older guys, who all peered at Tate with suspicion. I was feeling way too nervous to talk to anyone, but I did do my own hellos as we headed for the ice, and waited for drills, unsure of where I stood with the newest member of the Raptors. After all I was still on long-term injured reserve, not even part of this team, and he might think I wasn't worth talking to.

Shit. Pull yourself together. You're good at this hockey thing. You are worth people talking to you.

"You're fast," he announced after a moment's pause. "That move you pulled on the Vancouver goalie, the wraparound baseball move? That was so beyond fast, he never saw the puck coming." He extended a gloved hand, and I bumped it. "Want to practice on my wing?" He leaned in then, "I could do with the support right now."

Superstar Tate Collins remembered one of my moves? *And* he wanted me to practice on his wing? When it came to our turn, we left the wood board at speed, and we completed a couple of skates end to end, me pushing to outshine Tate, and ending up faster on the straight, Tate doing this whole Tate-thing where he took corners so fast that he caught up with me, and then we introduced a puck.

We were gold. With Ryker filling in the other side we were on fire. I somehow knew where Tate would be, and he had a sense of me.

It was poetry.

On our last run I stopped by the glass in front of Apollo and knocked it with my stick. He looked up from his Kindle and grinned at me, and I made a heart with my hands, although of course with the gloves it was difficult. He copied me, and I blew him a kiss which he pretended to catch and put into his pocket.

Apollo and I were our own kind of poetry and we fit. I just had to find a way to tell him what I was scared of. Then we could be happy forever.

Just find a way.

THIRTEEN

Apollo

HOW HAD IT HAPPENED?

How had the time gone so quickly? Where had it gone? Summer had raced past in an intoxicating blur of food, laughter, friends, and Henry. Sweet, blissful times loving each other, sunny days swimming or walking the grounds, watching him grow stronger and stronger, surer of himself, less reliant on me. I was overjoyed about his progress yet brokenhearted about it all at once. Yes, I'd fallen hard for the man despite my fragile heart warning me not to. Now it was time to extract myself from Henry's life and go back north. Back to Adler, the Railers, the short winter days and endlessly lonely cold nights.

While I'd packed my bags over the course of a week I'd told myself it was for the best. Logically, my brain knew that. Henry cared for me yes, and the sex was incredible, but he didn't love me, not in the way I needed. And so, as I gave the house a final cleaning on the morning of my flight back to Pennsylvania, I moved lethargically from room to room, taking time to touch everything in the hopes that I could commit every tiny detail to memory. Henry was at the practice arena working like a demon to secure his spot on the team. His new life, the one where he was solid, sure, confident, and secure, was at hand. It was time to let him fly.

Rucking the cushions around on the sofa in the TV room, thoughts swirling around me like a dust devil over desert sands, I found a small cookie wedged down between the back of the couch and the fat, soft seat. I plucked the smashed *Tortica de Moron* up and eyed the little Cuban treat in confusion. Then it came to me… the night that Henry and Bryan had talked, we'd been in here. The night we'd eaten so many of the guava and lime-filled cookies then had tussled over the one that I'd dropped. The night that I'd taken him into my body for the first time…

A rattling kind of sound burbled up from somewhere deep in my soul. I threw the cookie aside, leaving the tidying behind. I *had* to leave this house. Now. Not in five hours. Now. Before Henry came home. Before I had to look at his happy smile and listen to him telling me what a glorious future lay ahead. Maybe for him. Not for me. Six months I'd lived with and loved a man who didn't care for me as I cared for him. Not another day longer. I called Tía Sofía with shaking hands, tears tracking down my face. She came right away, racing out of a meeting, as I knew she would, and carted me and my bags to Tucson International Airport where one of the Lockhart fleet of personal jets sat waiting for me.

"Apollo, this isn't the way to do this!" Tía scolded as I

tugged on one of about ten bags wedged into the trunk of her red Jaguar XF. "What will Henry think when he gets home and finds you gone? He was supposed to see you off."

"I can't do it. That cookie was just... no. Fucking thing!" I jerked on the strap of my carry-on but it wouldn't budge. Tía Sofía, dressed in a red dress that matched the scarlet car, glowered at me and crossed her arms. "Ugh! Why are you just standing there?"

"Because I'm not going to help you run off like this. It's cowardly and our family aren't cowards."

"You drove me here! That makes you an accomplice. I know these things! I watch *How to Get Away with Murder*," I shouted as I jerked on that strap.

"I drove you here because you told me you had to fly out now because the jet had to go pick up Mrs. Lockhart when you were originally scheduled to take off." A plane took off, making talking impossible for a second. "If you'd have told me the truth when you called instead of once we reached the airport, I wouldn't have left work. This is not the way an adult handles things, Apollo. I'm very disappointed in you right now."

"So I lied! Sue me. Go ahead. You've got no idea what it's like to love someone who doesn't love you back!" I yelled up at her as cars pulled in, people got out, and cars left.

"Oh, baby, I've loved *lots* of men who wouldn't or couldn't love me back. I've also loved men who did, so I know that Henry does love you."

"No, no, he never said so. He doesn't love me and he

doesn't need me. Fuck you if you don't love me either." I turned from her to try another bag. This one wiggled free. Loading my arms with bags, and pulling two rolling suitcases behind me, I stormed into the airport, cheeks wet, and didn't look back at my aunt once. My heart was shattered, my soul bleak despite the brilliant sunshine warming Tucson. I marched along, chin up, and made my way to the fixed base operator terminal for those who were flying out with Lockhart Aviation. There were no security lines to wait in, no screaming kids, no waiting at all. I'd be on that sleek Lockhart AD34K and in the air in no time, leaving the pain behind me. Or so I'd thought.

It seemed jets needed to be fueled, and have shit done to them before they could take off. If I'd have been a few minutes earlier all would have been good, but five hours ahead of time meant that the plane was still due for preflight checks. And fuel. The pilot and co-pilot weren't even at the airport yet. There was one woman behind a glass-and-chrome desk who was only mildly freaked out about my early arrival.

"This is going to look so bad when it gets back to headquarters," she mumbled, while making calls to locate people to get me into the air with all due haste. "Adler Lockhart's personal assistant is here and ready to leave," she said into her Bluetooth headset, spinning from me. "I know he's five hours early, Tim, but what the hell am I supposed to do? Tell him to go fly commercial?"

"Miss, Miss, it's okay." I reached out to tap her shoulder. She whirled around, brown eyes wide as plates. "I'll wait. Tell the pilot that I'm happy to wait. I'm the one who screwed everything up by coming early."

"Thank you for being so understanding. We should have you in air in less than sixty minutes, Mr. Vasquez. We're so sorry."

I gave her my best smile. "Don't be sorry. This is all on me. I'm going to go get a drink at the Mexican restaurant in the main terminal around the corner. Text me when the plane is ready to take off." I gave her my info, left my bags with her, and made my way back out into the masses, the call of a pitcher of margaritas like a siren song. The interior of the Mexican place was shaded with thick hanging plants, the booths all packed, as were the tables. The hostess gave me a sorrowful look and a shrug.

"Can I get a drink and take it back to the Lockhart Aviation terminal, or whatever it's called?"

"Sure. What do you want?"

"A pitcher of margaritas." She blinked at me. "I'm expecting friends on the flight."

"Won't the jet have its own bar?"

Fuck. "Sure, yes, but we want to get an early start." Actually *I* wanted an early start. I hoped to be shitfaced when I landed in Harrisburg. Adler would have to carry me from the limo to our condo then I'd pass out, puke for three days, and slip back into the empty, cold life I'd left behind months before.

"Let me check."

I peeled off a hundred and handed it to her. "The change is yours."

Within three minutes I had a pitcher of tequila, orange liqueur, and lime juice all perfectly blended with ice. They even gave me a to-go plastic glass with salt on the rim. Juggling a full pitcher of cocktail and a salty tumbler, I began to weave my way through the throngs of travelers coming and going. I'd made it as far as the airport bookstore when I thought I heard someone calling my name. Since it wasn't a common name unless you were a Greek god living on Olympus, I paused, turned around carefully so as not to spill, and gaped at the sight of Henry barreling toward me, still in his hockey gear minus the skates, which had been replaced with Crocs. I lowered the pitcher I'd had over my head, my throat clogging with ten thousand emotions as he stumbled over an old woman in a purple hijab's suitcase on wheels, and nearly landed on his face.

"Henry, what the hell?" I asked when he righted himself.

"Sorry, ma'am, so sorry, I had to catch my boyfriend before he left town," he said to the irate Middle Eastern woman cussing him out in a lyrical, irate language. His sky-blue eyes flew to me as the woman wheeled off, still muttering.

Boyfriend.

He'd used that term. I'd never heard that word come out of his mouth before. "'Boyfriend'?"

"Yes, I mean, yeah, of course, if you want." He stepped closer, his hair dried in sweaty spikes, his face flushed. "I thought you knew."

"Knew? What? I just… how would I know? You never once told me that you thought of me as anything other than a buddy who you…" I glanced around at the kids and old folks. "A buddy who you did un-buddy like things with."

His shoulders drooped a bit, the big pads sagging. "I didn't know how."

"I… what? You just say it. I need a drink." I poured the tumbler full and took a swig, shuddered at the power of the tequila, and then downed half the glass in one long pull. "Here, hold this will you?" I handed the pitcher and glass off to some chubby dude in a Dungeons & Dragons T-shirt. Then I returned to Henry, who looked as if someone had just kicked his dog then ran over it then came back to knee him in the balls. "You just say it, Henry. Tell me what you feel. I need to hear it. I can't live here with you any longer being just friends with benefits. I want more."

"Do you love me?" His voice was soft, small, riddled with fear and doubt. My poor, sweet Henry. "You've never said it either."

"I have, Henry, in so many ways. Every time we make love I tell you. Every time I bake for you, or cook for you, every time I hold you close or play Scrabble or read beside you on the sofa, I'm telling you."

"That's bull. You're telling me that you love me in Spanish? That doesn't count! You know I don't speak that language! And you cook and bake for Adler, yet you don't love him like that, so this is just bullshit you running out on me when you do the same thing!"

Okay, he had me there. I wet my lips, the salty residue reminding me that my hundred-dollar pitcher of margarita was now… gone. Mother. Fucker. Ugh. That was *so* my life.

"Apollo, why are you leaving if you love me and I love you?"

I shrugged; my tongue suddenly unable to speak. Must have been the salt and the tequila.

He took a step closer, his arms rising slowly, his hands

cupping my face. My heart was pounding. "I should have told you but I was scared. You know what Aarni did to me…"

"And you know what asshole monkey ball face did to me."

"Yeah I do. But we're not them, right? We know better, know it hurts deep. We can do better. We *will*. Please, don't go. Stay here with me. I need you in my life. I… I love you so damn much. You're my light among all the shadows."

I leaned closer, rising to my toes. "I love you too. Please don't hurt me."

"I won't, I promise." His mouth moved over mine so gently I imagined it was a monarch butterfly alighting on a milkweed flower. "Promise not to hurt me?"

"Yes, yes, I promise so hard."

My arms went around his neck and he hoisted me clean off my feet, his mouth crashing over mine. Applause filled the air. Tears wet my face but I clung to him as if he were the only source of oxygen I had. And in a way he was. He was my life, my breath, my sunshine, and my boyfriend.

My boyfriend.

"Take me home. I want to be with you right now," I whispered when the kiss broke and the clapping died off. Henry was red-faced. "Take me home."

"Okay."

We bolted out of Tucson International, hand in hand, as if we had somewhere better to go than any place a stupid plane could take us. We did. Our house. The manse at the base of the mountains where we'd grown to know and love each other. Henry drove. I couldn't keep my hands or mouth off him as we made the forty or so minute drive. The driveway was too long, too bendy, the seatbelt too damn secure. He kissed me hard then popped my belt for me. I climbed over the console, squeezing my ass between his chest and the steering wheel, and captured his mouth. The horn blew loudly, scaring tiny shrieks out of us. He laughed. I licked into his mouth, wild for the taste of him.

"Mm, salty," he purred, cupping my ass. The horn sounded again. This time he reached down to find the lever for the seat. It flew back with a thud. I sat on his thighs, lapping at his mouth like a thirsty dog. His tongue twisted and danced with mine. We began yanking on clothes. Shirts were easy. Shorts and hockey pants not so much. "Inside. The bed. My bed, any bed."

"Yes okay, yes." We were half-naked before we were fully inside the house. Henry swept me up off my feet, the anklets I wore clattering, as did the bangles on my wrists. He carried me upstairs to his room and laid me on the bed, moving over me with power, muscles rolling and bunching, his eyes alight with lust and love. I nearly came then, seeing the affection in his gaze. "I love you," I said, in English, as I carded my fingers into his hair. "I trust you to always cherish me. Say you will. Tell me that you'll be mine and no one else's forever."

"Who could ever take your place? You're my sunshine. My only sunshine." I giggled at the silly old song then spread my legs for him.

He settled between my thighs, easing his cock alongside mine. I arched up, muttering tender little things in a mix of English and Spanish. Sweet nothings and dirty talk. "I love your cock. Your eyes make me think of summer days. Touch me again… again… again."

He eased into me, his prick sheathed and slick with lube. God, I loved this so much! The stretch, the tingle, the pressure of him filling me. His lips met mine. He kissed me thoroughly as he pushed deeper and deeper. I slid a leg around his lower back, the other resting on his calves. I licked at his lips then his jaw, down to his throat, picking up the zest of man and sweat.

"Slow, Henry, slow. I need this to go on forever," I begged, shoving my fingers into his hair as he flicked his hips.

"We'll be forever, I promise."

I might have cried then, would have, if not for the rub of his cock against that secret wonderful spot way inside. I gasped, clawed, shouted, and kicked at his ass with my heel. He drew out until I feared he'd be gone, then rolled his hips as he eased back into me. With a sharp toss of his hips, he hit my prostate again. Stars exploded at the base of my spine.

"More, please, more," I begged. He lowered his head, hands fisted on either side of my head, and he pumped slowly, moving his ass in that certain way and at that certain angle that wrecked me. He wiggled a knee under my ass, lifted me higher, then wedged a pillow under my backside, all while plowing me steadily. My arms fell from his shoulders, hitting the bed, fisting the covers. His fingers closed around my cock and he stroked it. I came in seconds, the orgasm rolling on and on, ribbons of cum covering my belly, chest, and chin. The tremors were fast, continuous, and robbed me of all coherent thought.

"So tight… so beautiful. Apollo… love you so much," I heard him growl then he was climbing up over me, going so deep I whimpered a bit. His cock kicked violently. My eyes rolled back into my head as his release hit him, leveling him like an unexpected twister in spring. His prick so deep breathing was tricky, I reached for him, grabbing his biceps then yanking him down over me, covering his mouth with mine. We rode out the shudders together, his weight on me a delight that I wanted to hold onto forever.

"I think I passed out," I gasped when the kiss ended. He rolled to the side, his arms around me, his cock sliding free. I shimmied over him, sealing my lips to his. "I love you," I whispered. He smiled, a lazy well-loved smile. My heart burst open and my insides were warm and sunny. "Stay with me, here, in bed. Please. All day. All night. Can you do that? Please? Just this once can hockey be second?"

"It will always be second," he said while stroking my stubbly cheek. "I'm yours for the day. I told Coach I had the runs, which I did. I had to run to get you after your Tía Sofía called me. Good thing we'd not been out on the ice yet and Coach didn't hear my phone."

"So that's how you knew I'd left early. She's always so pushy. I love her so much. Stupid cookie."

"Cookie?"

I'd tell him someday about the couch cookie, but not now. I kissed him hotly, and then kissed him once more, and then once more and once more and once more. We made love again, showered, and fell back into bed, mine this time. We stayed there all night long, touching and napping, tasting each other and waking up with him draped over me was scary yet amazing. I lay there listening to him breathe, his deep breaths flowing over the back of my neck. His leg lay over mine, his long arm was tight around my waist, almost as if he were scared I'd run off during the night.

My full bladder pulled me from the lingering fears trying to take over. I managed to get out from under him, tossed a sheet over his bare white bottom, and limped off to pee and find my phone. I had to call Adler and Tía Sofía. Explanations and apologies had to be made. My asshole was tender, like crazy sore, and my hamstrings ached. It felt marvelous, and yet not. I couldn't recall ever being this well-loved in my life. As I left the bathroom I heard my phone ringing.

Following the chirruping, I located my shorts in the front foyer along with Henry's hockey pants and his jock strap. There was a trail from the car to the bedrooms upstairs, and the front door was wide open. If there was a coyote or one of those peccary pig things in this house I would lose my shit.

"Hello," I said, eyeing the foyer with concern. What if a scorpion had snuck in, or a rattlesnake, or a roadrunner?

"It's about time, *mijo*. I've been calling you for hours." I frowned at the phone then looked at the time in the upper left corner. Shit. It was nearly eight. I ran to the front door, slammed it shut, and then raced upstairs to give Henry a shake. "Just in case you were wondering, I have your suitcases."

I skidded to a halt right outside my bedroom door. "Oh. Thank you, Tía." I'd kind of forgotten about them. "For the bags and for calling Henry and for so much more. I'm sorry I snapped at you. I didn't mean to say that to you."

"I know, baby. I'll let it go this time. The next time you tell your aunty to fuck off I will knock your pert ass to the floor, though. So tell me, did you and Henry work things out? Are you walking funny from all the talking and making up you two did all night?"

"*Si.*"

"That's my smart nephew. Now get back to that man of yours. I'll drop off your bags this afternoon. I doubt you'll need clothes anyway." I looked down at my dick swinging in the wind and sighed. She hung up while chuckling like the pervert she was. God above, I adored her. Smiling like a fool, I slid back into my bedroom to find Henry sitting up in my bed, hair tousled, neck peppered with love bites, eyes sparkling.

"Morning." I dumped the clothes and hockey pads onto the floor. Something inside the bundle began to vibrate. Since I had my phone it had to be his. "If you don't get a move on you're going to miss morning skate. I bet that's Ryker or Alex calling to remind you."

He grimaced at the thought. That made me snigger. I pawed through the pads, hockey socks, and underwear until his slim black Android buzzed inside his Raptors jersey. Pulling it free I leaped onto the bed, kissed him soundly, and then passed the phone over.

"If Coach kills me just know that I love you," he whispered then checked the voice mail that had been left. I wiggled in beside him, breathing in the smells of a warm Arizona day and the man I loved. I'd have to make a call myself later today to explain to Adler why I wasn't coming back to Harrisburg. That was going to be a hard call to make. I loved him so much but I loved Henry more. I prayed Adler would understand…

"Shit." I lifted my head from his shoulder. All the joy that had been on his face was now gone. His sky-blue eyes met mine. "It's from my mother."

FOURTEEN

Henry

"WHAT DOES SHE WANT?" APOLLO ASKED.

I could see his worried expression, and knew I probably looked worse. I passed him the phone and he read the text out loud.

"Could we meet up and talk?" He sat next to me and passed back the phone. "Will you?"

"I don't know." I had this nebulous thought that one day I would talk to her, but that was for a time much further in the future. A time when I wasn't feeling so hurt and raw and messed up. I turned off the phone, and placed it face down on the bedside table, then got out of bed and headed for the bathroom, Apollo close behind me. He sat on the vanity as I showered, he was next to me as I dressed, and he kissed me goodbye at the door. That was nice. Actually, it was beyond nice, and I hesitated at the car before stalking back and kissing him thoroughly. He hugged me hard and I headed to the practice arena for today's team workout. I'd only been driving again for a few weeks. It seemed odd to be behind the wheel;

empowering, but weird. I was used to Apollo being next to me driving and singing along to Madonna, and I missed his presence.

I should have said that last week, then maybe the airport scene would have been avoided, because I could have explained that I wasn't whole without him being there. Then there wouldn't be a clip on social media of me in full uniform pleading with Apollo while some guy in a Dungeons & Dragons T-shirt ran off with a pitcher of margaritas. I just hoped to hell no one at the Raptors had seen the video, but I probably wasn't going to be that lucky.

The parking at the arena was full, every single person there for training camp, all looking to prove that they deserved spaces on the final roster. There would be a mix of those offered tryouts, the skaters contracted, and those up from the Raptors feeder team, the Skylarks over in Sierra Vista. I wasn't guaranteed a place, I was only one year through my two-way rookie contract, and I could easily get put down to the Larks if I didn't shine today. Of course people like Vlad, Ryker, Alex, Colorado, and of course, Tate, they had nice contracts, or the skills to get one. I just hoped that I was up there with the best.

Believe in yourself, was what Lorraine had said.

I want you on my team, Vlad had announced and clapped me on the back so hard I'd nearly fallen over.

Suck it up and play hockey, Cyclops, was Colorado's advice. There were so many people in the locker room who'd heard him call me Cyclops that I knew damn well it would stick.

You're one of the fastest wingers in the NHL, you'll be

back, Ryker had told me, and Tate had nodded as if he agreed. Despite the fact that Tate coming in must have worried Ryker, he didn't let on, and Tate had deferred to Ryker on a couple of things last session.

Apollo didn't give me advice, he just said he wanted a season ticket to watch me play, and I knew he had blind faith, no pun intended, that I would make the final cut.

There was a space next to a rental car and I pulled in and killed the engine, climbing out with my gear and my game face on, then headed to the back door. There were some fans waiting, grouped in the shade of a wide awning, and I stopped to sign some autographs, and even talked to a couple of people about how good it was to be back.

Nerve-wracking, amazing, fear inspiring, terrifying, exhilarating, awful, exciting, I had all of those feelings jumbling around inside me, but all I could think of saying was that I was all good. Tate was taking far longer getting through the line of people; it seemed as if he had something personal to say to everyone, from the dads to the kids, to the moms, to the young women who hung off him as if he was a closet rail. I decided to rescue him, pulled him away, promised we'd come back out later, and then we were finally in the arena with the door shut behind us.

"Good save," Tate murmured.

"Wassup, Cyclops." Colorado fist bumped me. "Is it tequila time?" *Shit, he'd seen the damn video.*

"I'm not sure I like that nickname," I said with confidence. I don't know what it was about me recently but I was fighting for myself, and maybe this was the first thing to do.

Colorado cupped my shoulder, and brushed the hair off his face with the other. "No worries, dude, we'll just leave it as Cy, 'cause that is far easier." He left then, murmuring *Henry loves a boy.*

"I didn't mean…" There was no point in shouting after him, because that would just make everyone look at me, and I kind of wanted to go sit in my stall and mentally prepare myself. When I got to my space there was a plastic jug sitting there, filled with what seemed to be fizzy pop, and the label said *Tequila loving*. I picked it up and turned to face the room, but no one would look at me, the assholes.

"On the ice in twenty." Coach stopped me from saying what I was going to say, which wasn't going to be complimentary at all. His voice carried over the din of forty men cramped into space meant for less, and there was a hurried finishing of taping, rituals, and talking. With the fake tequila jug left behind, we were on the ice in ten, to a man, not wanting any black marks against our names. I was in the black jersey for today, along with Colorado, Tate, and a stern-looking Vlad. Ryker and the other guys in white were going to make today difficult, but if I could shine on Tate's wing, show Coach that all my training had paid off, and demonstrate that I had mad skills at being able to sense and focus, then I could make the cut, and show all those journalists who wrote about me and hockey being over, that they were wrong.

Three-on-three practice was intense, the black team edging out the white. Tate's line settled nicely, me on one wing, a new kid, Sam Bennett, called up from the Larks on his other. It wasn't just us, though. Colorado was down at the other end, and every time he blocked Ryker shooting, he would do this crazy cartwheel thing that I swear was going to get him in trouble.

Only Coach never said anything, but maybe he saw something in Colorado's crazy that the rest of us didn't.

Practice over, we headed back to the locker rooms, and the mood was high. Yes, we were going into next season with the label of a rebuild team, but we had Tate-freaking-Collins, Ryker, and Vlad-the-D-Man as our captain. I was desperate to get on this team, desperate for a second chance. Music blared from the speakers, some heavy rock that had Colorado on his knees in the middle of the room playing air-guitar.

"Henry? A word? And turn that music down!" Coach shouted from the door and then vanished in the direction of his office, and after a moment's hesitation in which my world crumbled around me, with the music volume dropping, I followed.

"Go, Cy," Colorado muttered as I passed.

I sent him a grateful look, then it was just me, Coach, and a closed door.

"Okay then," Coach Carmichael said and started to draw X's and O's on a flipboard. "See this? When Tate is…" His voice disappeared into nothing as I focused on the play he was detailing, something that Tate, Sam, and I had been playing with this morning. "… so yeah, that is what I think." He turned to face me, and I did try to keep standing, but when he frowned, I completely lost my cool.

"Am I going to make the team?"

He raised a single eyebrow, "What did I just say?" He thumbed at the flipchart, and I focused in on the marks.

"That Tate can blind pass, and I can… sorry, Coach, I wasn't listening." I didn't mean to sound so miserable, but that was what happened. "I think I'd gone into panic mode…" Should I have admitted that? I slumped into the nearest chair, sweat sticking my jersey to my skin, cooling and starting to stink, my skate guard caught on his desk, and god knows where I'd left my stick. *I'm a mess, I don't want to be, but I'm—*

"I said that I want you working with Tate, and that with you and him together, and possibly the Bennett kid, although that isn't definite obviously, although he shines, I think we could have an impressive first and second line for the season opener."

"Wait, you want me on the team?"

The frown reappeared, and this time he sat on his seat and wheeled it around to me, until our knees touched. He had such a kind face when he wasn't angry at us all for fucking up, or sternly trying to make the team better, his hazel eyes filled with compassion.

"Why do you think I got Lorraine to take you on? I literally begged management to fund that work, even though I didn't need to quite as much as Mark wanted me to have." He waggled his eyebrows, and I swear I flushed red. "They saw the same thing in you as I did. Ability. Strength. Jesus, kid, who else gets out of a car accident, half blind, and fights every single damn day to get back on the ice? It's been nothing short of a miracle, and yes, I can see areas for improvement, but you *will* be starting for the Raptors, and you will work your damnedest to prove to me that you are the fastest on this team, the most perceptive, and the sneaky charmer no one suspects can fight to the net. Got it?"

"Yeah, I mean, yes, I get it."

"Now go take a shower, you're stinking up my office, and not a word to anyone about my thoughts in here okay, or I will end you."

He was smiling, but I swear that he was more than capable of ending me. By the time I made it back to the locker room most of the guys had moved onto cool-downs, gym time, ability assessments, but Ryker and Alex were in there, along with Vlad and Colorado, and they looked at me expectantly. I wanted to tell them, I wanted to shout everything from the rooftops, I wanted to call Apollo and Dan and tell them, I wanted... so much.

Instead I smiled, and for my friends, that was enough.

Heading home was freaking joyful. I was exhausted, and grinning, and when Dan called, I connected the call as I pulled up at the house. *I will not tell him my news. I will not tell him my news.*

"Hey, how you doing?"

"I'm in love with Apollo and Coach said I'm making the team," I blurted. "Shit, you can't tell anyone yet, it's not... I mean, you can tell people about Apollo, but with the team, there's things that I have to... shit, Dan, I'm in love and I'm on the team!"

"Yes!" Dan shouted, and I could imagine him fist-pumping. We'd spent some time together over the summer, reconnected, made new memories, and he'd pointedly mentioned on several occasions about how good Apollo and I were together, and as to the whole skating thing, he'd been the loudest of my supporters, working with me on the ice sometimes, and convinced I would make it back.

"Mom texted me," I said, when he'd stopped whooping. The house door opened and Apollo stood there, looking all sexy and smiling hard.

"Yeah, I wondered if she would," Dan sounded cautious. "That's why I'm calling. She texted me too, I called her and she said that Ed isn't part of her life anymore. She's had counseling…"

"And?" I couldn't help sounding belligerent.

"And I'm flying out on Saturday, one day only, and meeting her. She suggested Tucson, I think because she hopes you'll come. I don't suppose you want to come with me, and see what she wants to say, maybe make it all three of us?"

Apollo held up a mug of what I assumed was coffee, and I put my fingers by my ear to let him know I was on a call. He vanished for a split-second, then appeared again, shirtless and flexing his body in all kinds of sexy poses. My mouth dropped open in the most comical way I could manage then I made a big show of covering my eyes, but actually peeked at him pouting on the steps.

"Henry, you still there?" Dan asked. Oh yeah, I still had a decision to make, and this one I had to make based on the silent entreaty in Dan's voice, and the fact that I wasn't an asshole, and if I was honest with myself, based on the fact that I really wanted to hear what Mom had to say.

"Yeah," I finally said. "Let's do this. When and where?"

"Saturday, Lucky's Diner. I'll text you the address."

WHEN I LEFT APOLLO IN THE CAR AND WALKED INTO Lucky's, Mom was already there, sitting opposite Dan. It seemed wrong to take the seat next to Dan as if we were interrogating her, but I was more comfortable there, than close enough for her to hug me.

"Hello," she said brightly. Her makeup was immaculate, her dress pretty, she looked younger than her age, and only if a person examined her really close, or knew her well, would they see the lines around her eyes, and the sadness in them. "It's so good of you both to meet me here."

The waiter arrived and I ordered coffee, but the thought of food in my churning stomach wasn't a good one. When he left Mom nodded, as if she'd been having a conversation in her head. "I owe you both an explanation, and I don't know how else to start but to say that lost my way," she began, and then cleared her throat. It seemed as if she was diving straight in and maybe that was for the best.

"Your dad and I... I loved him so much that when I was with him it was sometimes hard to breathe. He was everything to me, and when he died it broke me inside. I know it's not an excuse for what I did, but when Dan was drafted and left the house, I needed something for myself, to make that break hold together, and it was you, Henry, who bore the brunt of it. Then, when I met Ed, he seemed to have everything making sense for me. He made it seem as if he looked after me, but he was a manipulative liar, and by listening to him, I became less of a person because of it." All of that came out in a rush, as if she'd practiced the words. Not because they were lies, but because each syllable was ripped from a raw place inside her.

My chest tightened. She sounded like I did over Aarni.

"I'm sorry to both of you, for what I did, for who I became. I love you both so much, but I pushed you away," she placed a hand over Dan's and he stiffened. Then she touched me, and I was frozen to the spot. "And then I left you vulnerable, Henry, but the awful chasm inside me was filled with a grief so big it left me drained." Tears collected in her eyes, and next to me Dan sighed, then laced his fingers with hers. I wish it was that easy for me, but he had less to forgive. He'd left, and he wasn't the one who'd lost his money, and most of his childhood.

"Grief doesn't make you steal money," he said, sadly.

She winced. "I know." Silent tears welled in her eyes and spilled down her cheeks, but her voice was broken. "It wasn't me—"

"Your signature was on everything," I blurted and yanked my hand away from hers.

"So was yours," she pointed out softly, and I guess that was true. "Sorry, I didn't mean that to sound…" She was crying, and she had a point. I'd trusted that she was looking out for me, assumed it was her. *Was I wrong?* "I take full responsibility for what I allowed Ed to do, and I will take any punishment you think fits, just so one day I could be your mom again."

"You've always been my mom," I murmured. Coffee arrived and for a moment we stopped talking, but I could see that Mom had a lot more to say, and I was happy to sit and listen, just to attempt to understand.

"Thank you," she said, and squeezed my hand. "All those men in my life, all the men I wanted to be your dad, it just didn't work."

"Dad was unique," Dan whispered.

"I know, and I was looking for someone like him, always looking, and then I found Ed. Even though I knew he was never enough, I trusted him with my heart. All the time, I promise you that I tried so hard to keep you safe and happy before you left, but after, when I met Ed, I wanted him to be happy with me, and I gave all my trust and love to him. He stole from me, from us, I lost the house, that's gone, and worst of it all, he made me think he loved me, but he hurt me in so many ways. I know you shouldn't forgive me, or even understand what it was like to want someone to look at me the same way your dad did, someone who wanted me at the center of his world—"

"I get it, Mom," I interrupted her, and turned my hand palm up to lace our fingers. I had Apollo, and he made me the center of his world, and I knew I would be so lost if he wasn't there with me. After a short pause, Dan took her other hand and the three of us sat in silence.

"I get it," Dan added gently. "I have Anna, and Henry has Apollo. We get it."

"I'm so happy for you both, I swear, I couldn't hope for better. My only hope is that one day you boys can forgive me, for what I let happen. All your money, Henry, and Dan, I shut you out of my life, and Henry's."

Dan cleared his throat, "We're okay, Mom, we found our way back to each other."

I pressed my shoulder briefly against Dan. "We're good."

She pulled her hands free, and stood. "Maybe we could meet up again, one day, and try to fix fences, and you never know…" She picked up her purse, and I was thinking on my feet. She'd found Ed, I'd found Aarni, and both of us had suffered. A fierce protectiveness welled inside me, and I had to stop her from leaving. Yes, there was a lot to get past, and tons of forgiveness to dredge up, but it was a start.

"Apollo is in the car waiting," I began softly. "I know he'd love to meet you, and he makes awesome cocktails. Why don't the three of us go back to my place, and see if we can't talk some more?"

Dan threw some bills down to cover the coffee and Mom pressed a hand against her mouth as if she wanted to cry out loud.

"That would be wonderful," she whispered.

And somehow in that single moment in the diner with possibly the worst coffee in history, there was a glimmer of hope that the Greenaway family would start to heal.

Epilogue

APOLLO

"Phew. Right, You can do this, Apollo." I glanced up from my tablet, resting on my new pink iPad pillow holder, at Henry doing some late afternoon laps in the pool. Sweet Mother Mary, his body was a divine creation if I'd ever seen one. I took a sip of the now daily batch of *Agua de Jamaica*, the ice cubes tickling my upper lip, then returned to the task at hand. "You can do this. If Henry could bring his mother here yesterday to talk and make up, you can do this."

And so I hit up Adler online. A video chat seemed to be the best way to handle it. A text or email seemed impersonal. He answered quickly, his face coming so close to his phone I could see up his nose.

"Oh hey, it's Apollo Vasquez! Foxy, you can call the Pennsylvania State Troopers and tell them we found our missing person," he shouted over his shoulder. "Seems he was just lost in a vacuum cleaner factory for close to two days." Shit. I'd forgotten to use cover-up on the love bites on my neck. I hurried to pull my see-through poolside shawl up to my neck. "Yeah, that sheer little wrap isn't really hiding the hickeys."

I huffed. Adler dropped his phone from his eyeball and sat there at the kitchen island—I knew that condo of his well—giving me a glare that would've scared other people. I drew in a breath through my nose, let it out, and then began my well-rehearsed speech.

"I'm sorry for not making that flight. And I'm sorry for not touching base before now, there's been a lot going on out here and I was swept up. I promise I will never stand you up like that again. You must have been worried sick."

"Not really. I called Tía Sofía when I got the call that you'd not shown up for the charter at your end. She told me you and Henry were 'talking about your relationship', which we both know is code for fucking like horny hippos."

"I… she… you two are so… Ugh!" Adler chuckled. "Okay, well, I'm glad you called her. I felt so bad for not contacting you."

"It's cool. I know how it is to be in love." He gave Layton a goofy smile as he pattered past behind Adler with a coffee cup and his nose in his phone. "So, are you ever coming home?"

I looked out over the grounds, at the old pool house sitting idly about a hundred or so feet from where Henry was doing laps. The winds whistled down the mountains, warm still, filled with sweet floral scents and perfectly dry air. The sun was on my head.

"No, I'm not coming back." I chanced a peek at my best friend in the world, fearing he'd be frowning or mad, or maybe even crying. He was smiling. Sure, his eyes were a little dewy, but he was smiling.

"I figured that when I saw you and Henry together. He loves you a lot, buddy. And it's so easy to read you."

"I'm not that easy to read," I argued weakly.

"For me you are. Hey, look here at me and not at the roadrunners."

I did as he asked, wiping at the tears welling in my eyes. "I feel as if I'm letting you down. I know you depend on me and I'm just… I'm walking away from you to be here and that's so greedy and… and—"

"Hey, hey, no *way* are you doing that. Listen to me, Apollo. I'm a grown-ass man, close to turning thirty. If I can't manage to feed myself and pay my own bills by now someone should slap me upside the head." Layton slapped him upside the head. I snorted so hard my sinuses vibrated. "Ouch! Okay, fine, so I'm not quite there yet but I will be with Foxy Man here to help me grow up."

"Oh God no, don't ever grow up! We love you just like you are." Adler rolled his eyes then got a tender kiss from his man before Layton slipped out of the camera's eye. "I do love Henry. So much. And he loves me too. We've got some work to do on communicating what we need and want, but we'll get there. I want to stay here, in Arizona. I love it here, the people, the weather. I want to see where life takes us, me and Henry."

"Excellent. I'm super happy for you. I'll find a pen and the deed and sign the house over to you as a He's-Found-His-One-True-Love gift! Foxy, where's that pen I bought you when we were sparking?"

"No, Adler, no. Stop." He looked from his man to me.

"No, I don't want that. Well, I mean I do but…" I paused to gather my thoughts. "Okay, so, I've been thinking about doing something more meaningful with my life. Now that Henry is healed up he doesn't need me as a companion anymore. Which means I'm back to having nothing to do with my time. So, I've been thinking of going to college out here, maybe get a degree in physical therapy or be a home health nurse. I get real satisfaction helping people heal."

"You'd be a frigging awesome home health nurse, Apollo. People just love you. Go for it. I'll pay for your schooling. No, don't make that face. Have you told your mother?"

"Not yet, I will. I need to have things all in place." He nodded. He knew all too well. Mama hadn't hesitated to punish both of us when we were kids. "I'm trying to talk her into moving out here but so far, well, you know how she is. Anyway, I don't need your money for college. You've paid me enough to send five people to school for years. I've got the cash in the bank for my courses. It's the house I want to talk to you about."

"It's yours! Foxy Man, where are you with a pen?"

"Adler, no, I… please, hear me out."

"Do you not want the house? Is it not what you like? I can have it redone, just say the word."

"Adler, no, focus." I had to smile. He truly was like an Irish Setter puppy at times. "Okay, so the thing is, this mansion is perfect. It's just too big for two people. It could be put to much better use as a recovery center for athletes who have suffered a catastrophic injury. Kind of like a halfway house, you know. Where me and some other health professionals could work with them as they transition from the formal rehab centers to the actuality of real life."

"That's fucking *amazing*! I'll happily donate the house to this new halfway house of yours. I *really* need a pen and a lawyer now. *Foxy!* Oh, there you are. Can you find the deed to the house in Tucson? And a real estate attorney on my speed dial? Apollo and Henry are going to turn the desert house into a halfway home for rehabbing athletes. Oh, and Apollo is going to college to be a nurse, or maybe a physical therapist! Also, like you and me both said, he's not coming back to Harrisburg. He's got a new man, a good one this time."

Layton slipped up behind Adler, rested his scruffy chin on Adler's shoulder, and then gave me the warmest smile. "Congratulations on all fronts, Apollo. We knew you and Henry would end up together. And I love the idea of a halfway house for rehabbing athletes. I bet that transition is tough for a lot of them, but if the house is turned over to the new foundation, where will you and Henry live?"

"In the pool house." I stood, put my pillow tablet holder on the lounge, and swung my tablet around so they could see the pool, Henry plowing back and forth like a dolphin, and the abandoned pool house. When the camera was back on me, I padded down the steps to the pool area, the puddles on the hot concrete under the hot Arizona sun. "It's perfect for a new couple. It's got three bedrooms, and two full baths, so if Mama comes to visit she can stay with us. A full kitchen so I can cook, a TV room, and a gym. We've been inside and… well, we fell in love with it. So, if you're willing to donate the house for a charity then we can start moving on with our dreams out here."

"Of course I'll donate the house to charity. I already told you that. Is there anything else you need? Beds? Band-Aids? Bed pans?"

I laughed at his exuberance then sat on the edge of the pool, letting my feet slip into the cool water at the deep end. Henry swam over to rest his arms on the rounded edge of the cement. His eyes were bright, his smile soft and warm, and his love for me radiated out of him.

"Yes, but not now. Right now we just need your permission to go ahead and begin setting things up. Oh, and a few lawyers to help do it would be nice."

"Consider it done! All I ask is that you name it after me." Layton began to sputter. "Easy, Foxy Man, easy. I was kidding. You knew I was kidding, right, Apollo?"

"Yeah, I knew you were kidding. I love you, Adler. My brother."

"I love you too, buddy. Go. Be happy. Live your life with the man you love. Honestly, my brother, there is *nothing* better than being with your soul mate."

I nodded because talking was out of the question. I was so happy. So damn happy and crying good tears. We ended the call. Henry pushed up out of the pool, took the tablet from my shaking hands, laid it on a glass table between two white metal chairs, and scooped me up from the side of the pool as if I weighed nothing. Which was a lie because my rompers were all tight across my ass.

"Oh! Don't drop me." I squeezed his neck tightly, watching the mansion growing farther and farther away.

"Where are you taking me? Our beds are back that way!" I jerked my chin in the direction of the airy manse.

"I'm taking you to our future."

He nudged the door of the pool house open with his elbow then stepped inside. It was dusty and smelled as if it had been shut up for years, which it had. But a day with the windows open would clear out the signs of a house sitting vacant. Then he kissed me soundly, our love, like the sweet Arizona sun, chasing the last lingering shadows from our lives.

The End

Next for the Raptors

Sugar And Ice (Raptors 4)

Tate Collins used to be the highly marketable face of Dallas hockey. With charity work, good deeds, friending rookies, and working closely with the local children's hospital, he was good and perfect and an all-American nice guy. Until under pressure to conform, he proposes to his current girlfriend, who then decides that he is her ticket to fame and fortune. When she signs up for the new season of a hockey wives reality show, she shares things his team mates had told him in private, and in doing so exposes more of him than he ever wanted people to know. As the fact that he cried with *Titanic*, or that he has a huge collection of *Star Wars* figures, or worse, that he had a secret crush on Tennant Rowe.

Traded to the Arizona Raptors, he arrives determined to make it work and resolving to make a difference. Until, that is, he arrives in the locker room, and realizes that he doesn't fit in. Not only do puck bunnies swarm him at every turn, but no one on the team will talk to him about anything but hockey, they never ask him out for team meals, and prank him at every turn. The only person who seems to trust him is the icy Russian D-man, Vlad, but not even that support is making things work with the team. Tate knows something has to change, but maybe falling for the captain of the team wouldn't be Tate's best move.

Vladislov Novikov has been called many things over his long and illustrious career, but the nickname of Iceberg seemed to stick best. Perhaps it's due to his icy blue eyes, or the way he rams into opposing players as he defends his goalie or teammates. Maybe it's because of his cool demeanor when not playing the game he loves. Vlad wouldn't say he's cold-hearted, he's just guarded and discreet, picking lovers much like himself: mature, self-possessed men who are willing to let him be in charge when things get rough. Which is why he's the perfect team captain for this wild bunch of puck-pushers.

Life is smooth as ice until Tate Collins rides into Tucson with his boyish charm, his captivating smile, his apple pie ways, and those damn dimples. The young superstar immediately catches his discerning eye, and despite knowing better than to start something with a teammate, the big, bad iceberg is about to have that chilly wall around his heart melted away by Tate one sweet kiss at a time.

Hockey Series' from RJ Scott & V.L. Locey

Harrisburg Railers

Owatonna U Hockey

Arizona Raptors

Boston Rebels

LA Storm

Chesterford Coyotes - Young Adult

*When hockey wunderkind Tennant Rowe meets his new coach, he
knows he's in trouble. Jared Madsen is nine years older than
Tennant, impossibly attractive, and — worst of all — his
brother's off-limits best friend. Is their chemistry worth the risk?*

Changing Lines (Railers 1)

Can Tennant show Jared that age is just a number, and that love is
all that matters?

The Rowe Brothers are famous hockey hotshots, but as the
youngest of the trio, Tennant has always had to play against his

brothers' reputations. To get out of their shadows, and against their advice, he accepts a trade to the Harrisburg Railers, where he runs into Jared Madsen. Mads is an old family friend and his brother's one-time teammate. Mads is Tennant's new coach. And Mads is the sexiest thing he's ever laid eyes on.

Jared Madsen's hockey career was cut short by a fault in his heart, but coaching keeps him close to the game. When Ten is traded to the team, his carefully organized world is thrown into chaos. Nine years his junior and his best friend's brother, he knows Ten is strictly off-limits, but as soon as he sees Ten's moves, on and off the ice, he knows that his heart could get him into trouble again.

Changing Lines

Harrisburg Railers (Hockey Romance)

13. Family First

Railers Volume 1 | Railers Volume 2 | Railers Volume 3 | Railers Volume 4

Meet the men of Owatonna University's hockey team

Ryker (Owatonna U, 1)

Ryker

Ryker is hockey royalty, Jacob is a poor country boy. Can two vastly different people find common ground and become the men they want to be?

Ryker comes from a long line of championship-winning hockey players. Playing college hockey to develop his game is his only focus, and nothing will stand in the way of him working to become the best player. He has no room for relationships, people who point out his flaws, or anyone who calls him on his dreams. He certainly has no place for love, and meeting Jacob is nothing but a useful distraction on the side. After all trying to get his Owatonna Eagles teammate into bed is less work and more play. When tragedy rocks his family, his charmed life crumbles, and the only person he can turn to is the same one who claims to hate him.

Jacob Benson has only known hard work and stifling conservative values his whole life. Born and raised in the small rural community of Eden Crossing, Minnesota, he's the only son of a hard-working but struggling dairy farming family. Jacob is using his skills in hockey to finance his way to an agricultural science degree. These four years at Owatonna U. will probably be the only time he has to enjoy life, gain acceptance about his sexuality, and live openly before his inevitable return to the farm. Running into a pretty rich boy like Ryker Madsen is putting a damper on his enjoyment of life away from home. Ryker's flip, conceited, carefree attitude grates on Jacob's every nerve. So why, if Ryker is everything he dislikes, does he want nothing more than to explore the sinful dreams that his annoying teammate stars in every night?

Ryker

Owatonna U Hockey (Hockey Romance)

1. Ryker
2. Scott

Coast to Coast (Arizona Raptors 1)

Coast To Coast

When opposites attract, this bottom-of-the-league team will never be the same again.

A stipulation in his father's will forces Mark back into the arms of a family that disowned him and leaves him one-third owner of a hockey team facing financial ruin. He doesn't even watch hockey, let alone like it, and wants nothing more than to head back to New York. Then there's the new coach, a stubborn, opinionated, irritating man with superiority issues and questionable music taste. Butting heads with Rowen becomes the new normal, but it comes with passionate debate and an all-consuming lust.

Challenged to rebuild one of the worst teams in the league into a future cup contender, Rowen can't pass up the opportunity. Never in his twenty years of hockey has he ever seen a team managed so badly or coached players overflowing with resentment and bigotry. Yet there's something about this team and this city that compels him to roll up his sleeves and start dismantling. If only Mark, one of three siblings who now own the Raptors, wasn't so damned rock-headed yet so damned appealing his job might be easier. It doesn't look like either is willing to give in, but one night in a dark, desert hotel changes everything.

Coast To Coast

Arizona Raptors (Hockey Romance)

1. Coast To Coast
2. Across the Pond
3. Shadow and Light
4. Sugar and Ice
5. School and Rock

Boston Rebels

Top Shelf (Boston Rebels 1)

Top Shelf

Acting on the attraction to his best friend's brother has always been off the table for Xander until a passionate hookup with Mason at a beach resort begins a love affair that burns long after summer ends.

Mason specializes in assisting same-sex couples on their journey to becoming parents and fighting every rule that blocks his way in the stuck-in-the-past agency that hired him. Living in his brother's pool house is rent-free, and every cent he earns he saves for his dream—that one day he'd have his own company helping others. The downside is that he has to see his annoying brother every day, the upside is that his brother's teammates from the Boston Rebels make regular visits. The eye candy that passes Mason's window is almost enough to make him consider dating a hockey player, but not just any player though. Ever since Xander —his brother's childhood friend—came out as gay at a press conference, Mason's puppy love has turned into a burning attraction he can no longer ignore.

Hockey has been one of Xander's main focuses since he was old enough to balance on skates. Well, hockey and Mason Kingsley, but Mason was always unattainable. Now that he's about to see thirty candles on his birthday cake and is no longer hiding the fact he's gay, he's ready to find a soul mate to make his life complete. A summer vacation is just what he needs to have time to think, but when the Boston Rebels arriving in paradise with Mason in tow, thinking is the last thing he needs. One torrid night under a balmy moon and rules about not messing with his best friend's brother vanish on a warm, tropical breeze.

Summer romances don't generally last past Labor Day, but with the new season about to begin Xander and Mason are going to have to face the world and decide if their love is real enough to withstand everything.

Top Shelf

Boston Rebels

Lost In Boston (Free Prequel Novella)

1. Top Shelf
2. Back Check
3. Snowed
4. Royal Lines
5. Blade
6. Rental

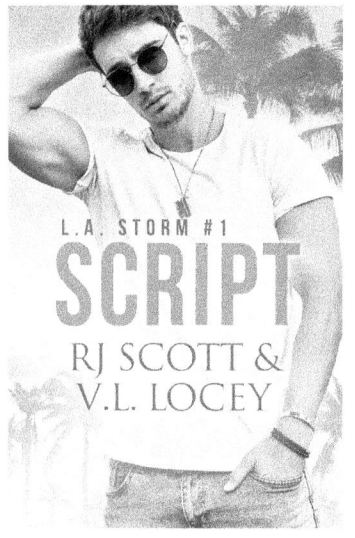

Script (LA Storm, 1)

Script

Hollywood A-lister Finn might be Canadian, but he needs Cameron to show him how to hockey.

Actor Finn Kerrigan is at a crossroads. After growing up a soap star, then starring in a hugely successful trilogy of action movies, he's finally given the chance to read a heartfelt and passionate script that could change his life forever. The role would be enough for people to see him as a serious actor, and maybe even win him an award or two (and no, a golden raspberry award for his action movies doesn't count). Once established as a serious actor he's sure he can come out of the closet and finally live his truth. When he lies to get the part of a hockey player on a struggling team, he suddenly has nowhere to hide. He might be Canadian, but the last time he skated he was ten, and no, he doesn't have hockey in his blood. With only a month until filming starts, he about to be exposed, but partnered with a player who's supposed to be giving him tips, he doesn't realize how many of his secrets will come to light. Falling in lust, one heated kiss at a time, is inevitable, but giving Cameron up at the end of the shoot could break his heart.

Cameron Chavkin is the face of the LA Storm. And the body, and the hair, and the smile. He's at the prime of his career, men and women want to be with him, and he's skating better than he ever has before. His house sits next to a famous rock star's mansion, his garage is filled with expensive cars, and he's even been asked to mentor a once-famous actor in a new hockey movie. Life is pretty sweet. Until the bad boy of hockey meets Finn, a man on the edge with more secrets than Cameron has endorsements. Knowing better than to get involved, Cameron is swept up despite himself, and when it's time to say goodbye to the Storm's most eligible bachelor is finding it hard to follow the script.

Script

LA Storm

4. *Spiral*

Chesterford Coyotes, Young Adult
Romance

Off The Ice (Chesterford Coyotes, 1)

Off The Ice

**A coming-of-age love story with high school, hockey rivalry,
friendship, family, and coming out.**

Soren's life changes in an instant when he and his younger
brother are adopted by hockey royalty. Making sense of his new
life is hard enough, but when he's enrolled in a private school it
means facing a whole new set of problems. Navigating
friendship, family, and hockey is one thing, but being attracted to
the boy who vexes him is a whole new thing.

Felix has a reputation to protect. He's the kid who seems to have everything but looks can be deceiving. Spinning lies about his perfect life, he's created a fantasy world that even he has started to believe. Only, it's not long before everything crumbles, all of his pretty lies are revealed, and only his closest rival sees through his pain and stands by him.

Fighting is easy, friendship is hard, but love is everything.

Off The Ice

Chesterford Coyotes

Also By RJ Scott

For a full list of ebooks and links please scan the code above or visit rjscott.co.uk/rjbooks

Meet RJ Scott

RJ discovered romance in books at a very young age and realized that if there wasn't romance on the page, she could create it in her head. With over one hundred and fifty books published, she is a full time author of gay romance.

She lives and works out of her home in the beautiful English countryside, spends her spare time reading, watching films, and enjoying time with her family.

The last time she had a week's break from writing she didn't like it one little bit and has yet to meet a box of chocolates she couldn't defeat.

www.rjscott.co.uk | rj@rjscott.co.uk

NEWSLETTER - rjscott.co.uk/rjnews

facebook.com/author.rjscott

x.com/Rjscott_author

instagram.com/rjscott_author

amazon.com/author/rj-scott

bookbub.com/authors/rj-scott

goodreads.com/rjscott

pinterest.com/rjscottauthor

Also By VL Locey

For a full list of ebooks and links please scan the code above or visit vllocey.com/stories-from-vl-locey

Meet V.L. Locey

V.L. Locey loves worn jeans, yoga, belly laughs, walking, reading and writing lusty tales, Greek mythology, the New York Rangers, comic books, and coffee.

(Not necessarily in that order.)

She shares her life with her husband, her daughter, one dog, two cats, a flock of assorted domestic fowl, and two Jersey steers.

When not writing spicy romances, she enjoys spending her day with her menagerie in the rolling hills of Pennsylvania with a cup of fresh java in hand.

vllocey.com
vicki@vllocey.com

Newsletter - vllocey.com/newsletter

facebook.com/V.L.Locey
x.com/vllocey
instagram.com/vl_locey
bookbub.com/authors/v-l-locey
goodreads.com/vllocey
pinterest.com/vllocey